T0158785

Also by John Ricks

Freddy Anderson's Home:
Book 1 in the Freddy Anderson Chronicles

Protectress: Book 2 in the Freddy Anderson Chronicles

Sword and Sorcery: Short Stories Book 1

COLOSSUS

Freddy Anderson Chronicles
BOOK 3

BY

John Ricks

 iUniverse®

COLOSSUS
FREDDY ANDERSON CHRONICLES BOOK 3

Copyright © 2016 John Ricks.

All rights reserved. No part of this book may be used or reproduced by
any means, graphic, electronic, or mechanical, including photocopying,
recording, taping or by any information storage retrieval system
without the written permission of the author except in the case
of brief quotations embodied in critical articles and reviews.

This is a work of fiction. All of the characters, names, incidents,
organizations, and dialogue in this novel are either the products
of the author's imagination or are used fictitiously.

iUniverse books may be ordered through booksellers or by contacting:

iUniverse
1663 Liberty Drive
Bloomington, IN 47403
www.iuniverse.com
1-800-Authors (1-800-288-4677)

ISBN: 978-1-5320-0705-7 (sc)
ISBN: 978-1-5320-0706-4 (e)

Library of Congress Control Number: 2016917298

Print information available on the last page.

iUniverse rev. date: 11/14/2016

To veterans. Thank
you so very, very much
for your service.

INTRODUCTION

✦ ✦ ✦

Freddy is still in the clutches of the alien kidnappers, and things are heating up. The human race goes to war to help a benevolent race that has been helping them since before written knowledge. Humans are now at war with a race that is looking to destroy everything in its path—and Earth is directly in the way. Freddy helps in every way he can but at a cost that nearly drives him insane. Then his love gets kidnapped and viciously taken away. She is in a deadly trap, and only a miracle can save her.

P R O L O G U E

✦ ✦ ✦

I was still on the alien ship, in a tank designed to hamper my mental abilities, being cerebrally scanned by the green creature. The green alien was sending everything from my past to a big monitor directly above my head and to several other monitors attached to strange-looking equipment for observing vital statistics and other medical purposes. The ship was moving through space at top speed, heading toward their planet. Several other creatures surrounded the tank I was in. A big Gray stood there, loaded down with blasters and a wicked-looking long blade. His eight arms were crossed, as if he were upset, and his facial expression— pursed lips and squinted eyes—was one of irritation. I read his emotions as great concern tinged with excitement and a little fear. A Blue stood to my left. His head was raised, with chin up, as if to show he was above the rest; his eyes, however, moved too much, quickly darting here and there, showing he was fearful about something. His eight hands were clasped together as if to keep them from giving away that he was deeply afraid. Twin little yellow aliens were using their arms together to hold me up in the tank. They acted as one in all their movements, and they spoke the same words together when they talked, as if they were one creature. Other green and purple aliens were scattered around the room, keeping busy at the equipment.

✦

Two big yellow aliens walked into the room and, in one mixed, harmonic voice, asked Gray, "How is the battle going?"

Gray furiously answered, "They know our strengths and weaknesses now. Tapping into our computer gave them enough information to be nearly our equals in battle. They are an angry race, and they want their hero back immediately. They are using weapons that we did not know they had. Half our fleet was destroyed in minutes. We have asked for a momentary truce. We have found out that they are not worried about winning or losing. Five other races are giving them support and mobilizing for battle. Soon, the sky will be filled with their ships. We are, for the first time, in trouble."

Little Yellows added, "They have only one demand of us. 'Give us back our Freddy.' It is their only request. We have told them why we attacked and what we found out, but they know we have been stealing their people for many years and gathering information. They are sorry for mistakenly destroying our ship, but they believed we were going to attack anyway. They asked what type of 'mother ship' they destroyed. Their 'specials' are very talented and knew before we answered."

In a panic, Green asked, "They know it was an invasion?"

Little Yellows said, "Yes, and now Freddy knows. Thank you." They moved their tentacles tighter around my head before saying to me, "It is our race's belief that we should dominate the universe."

I said, "Then you will fail, for it is built into our race not to be dominated." I shut my mind down.

Blue said, "We have little time before they restart their attack. Green, please continue."

Green said, "I cannot. He has found a way to close his mind completely to me."

Little Yellows said to me, "Open your mind, little one, or be tickled."

I kept my mind closed but lost concentration when the tickling started. "Darn."

Green smiled. "Shall we continue, then? Thank you, Yellows."

C H A P T E R   1

✦ ✦ ✦

BEGUILED

I awoke from a sound sleep, remembering all the wonderful things I had seen while on vacation. Disney World and the Smithsonian were great. I could have done without the press conferences, and the politicians actually made me ride in a ticker-tape parade. That was horrible, wet, and cold, and thousands of bits of paper stuck to my hair. I received lots of presents and things that I had to return. What would I do with a luxury BMW? I won't be of legal driving age for three more years. I must admit that I was treated really nice, but underlying thoughts were *He could make me rich* and *What if he's reading my mind?* It was really good to get back home and away from all the wide-open minds. I wonder how Tammy's handling the move to home.

I bounced up and out of bed to get dressed. All this work crafting ships to save the world created a lot of muscle—my body is a fully toned and chiseled tool—so I bounced too far. My now very long blond hair caught on the bedpost, and I fell to the floor. *Ouch!* I stood up and untangled my hair. This was not a good way to start the day; perhaps I need another vacation. It's been a year since that last vacation. This was going to be a big day for me. I was finished with

"One of the little benefits of being guarded," Katie said as she sat down across from me.

"I know, Katie. There are a lot of benefits. Like not getting shot by that nut last month, not breaking my neck, and not blowing myself up, but I would still like to be alone sometimes."

"I know. So would I."

"I have a great idea. Why don't we take a ship and leave? We could go hide somewhere and play pirates."

She laughed. "That would be a great idea, but where could we go and be hidden? Now that the world has your scanners there is no place to hide."

"Oh, I can fix that. Besides, the scanners have a limited range."

She frowned at me, and I could tell she was upset by the tone of her voice. "Freddy, don't you dare. Besides," she said accusingly, "I thought you said the scanners could not be fooled?"

I laughed. "I said *you* could not fool them. I didn't say I couldn't."

"Leading us to believe something that's not true is still lying. You knew that when you said it. So stop." More gently, which put me on guard, she asked, "Does this have anything to do with your secret project? When can we see it?"

I quickly tightened my shields, as I don't like giving my secrets away early. "This is a very good sandwich. Want a bite?" I held it out to her with an innocent look.

"You've got something big back there," she said with a grin. "How long will it be before you bring it out?"

I smiled at her. "Remember who taught you the trick of getting people to think about something for which you want information. Please don't think it's going to be that easy with me, Katie."

"Very well. You win—for now—but you're making Captain James extremely nervous."

I was supposed to be a super-genius, but Captain Susan James could talk me into anything. She convinced me to accept her help—and therefore, the help of the entire world— and then had me willingly turn my home into a naval base. She's the smartest person I've ever met. She's kind to a fault, unless you make her mad. She's tall, muscular, and a born leader. She keeps her blonde hair in short, tight curls—it makes her look more male than female—and I love her like a mother. I said, "Katie, Susan can wait until I'm ready."

"Very well, but she's planning to talk to you about it soon."

"Thanks for the warning." I said, smiling and planning to avoid Susan at all costs. "Time to go to work."

"Don't stay in there long, Freddy. You have a lot to do today."

"I won't." I headed toward the shop. It used to be easy. Just go outside and walk unobstructed to the entrance. Now I have to go around several rows of houses and at least three guards, and I get challenged at the door. I'd skip all that by teleporting inside the shop, but with all the new specials at the base I had to make that impossible, even for me. "Specials" are a nice way to refer to kids with mental talent. Then again, I could use the new teleportation device in my room, as it's connected directly to the shop, but I don't want to give that away yet. I shielded all the walls in the mountain in a way that made them completely impregnable to all forms of mental dabbling, unless I approved it. As I finally was walking up to the entrance—what do you know?—Tammy was there, just checking out with the guard. "Good morning," I said to the guard.

"Good morning, Dr. Anderson." The guard had already scanned me as I approached, so the guard knew it was me.

I turned to Tammy and lovingly said, "Good morning, Tammy. How was your night?"

"It was fine, sweet cakes." She walked closer to me, and I swear my knees went weak. As she walked past, I turned to follow her in a daze, but the guard got my attention by grabbing my arm and forcing me to focus on her. I swear, for a moment I'd forgotten everything I was doing.

"How many people in the shop this morning, Sue?" I asked the guard.

"About eighty, sir. It's the graveyard shift. You need to stay away from Tammy, sir! That girl is not good for you."

Interestingly, when she made the comment about Tammy, something in her voice seemed to border on hatred.

She asked, "Are you going in?"

"Yes."

She touched a button that allowed two-way communications with the inside. "Dr. Anderson is coming in. Open, please."

The shield covering the entrance dropped. They had taken out my switch and added a computerized and highly protected software so that no one with telekinetic abilities could trip it and walk in—another required change. I walked in through the front offices and into the open building room and paused to look over the gigantic space. Then I took the lift down to the main floor and went right past all the ships, robots, and people, saying hi and good morning to them all. Some I recognized, but many I did not. Where had all my plans gone? I was supposed to approve each person working here. Oh yes. I remember. Susan talked me out of that, saying that it was a waste of my time, now that they had the right checks in place. We also have a staff of over twenty specials on the base. The oldest is twenty, and the youngest is four, and I am still, by far, the strongest. That rankles me to no end. There should be others who have much more power than I have. It just isn't fair, as everyone looks up to me, and that causes Susan to be harder on me—she says I'm their idol, so I should "be good." I don't want to be anyone's idol. I just want to invent and build. For some reason, I've been upset a lot lately.

I went back to my secret rooms and thought about why I was feeling so bad about things. I approved most of them. I had control to a very large extent. "Shop?"

"Hi, Freddy. What can I do for you?"

"How many items do I still need to patent?"

"Only 523. They're all in this section of the shop. You haven't told anyone about them, so the paperwork has not been started."

"Really. What's my gross income looking like?"

"You're taking in over one billion dollars a week and spending only 123 million."

I'm in the black. Cool. "How much on my to-do list?"

"Eighty-one items."

"Thank you."

That is a big change from the millions of to-do items I had just one year ago. I should be elated. So why am I upset over my situation? I like the people I am working with. I like the specials. Most have good personalities, except Tammy.

Tammy—what a person. Her specialty is drawing men's attention. Well, not really. It's empathy, and she's strong. She can spot a lie before the first word is out of your mouth, and she has no problem letting you know not to say it. It's just that she's so shy and pretty and kind and very easy to talk to that I'm jealous when she's with other men. Yet I love Becky! So why am I always thinking of Tammy, just like the rest of the men on this base? *That's it!* I'm just as bad as the rest of the men on this base, and I'm only thirteen years old. I can't stop thinking about Tammy, and when I'm not around her, I get upset. She has to be the reason why all the men are running around, ready to fight all the time. Even I'm upset,

"One priority message from Chief Henry Peters and one relayed through Shop from Freddy."

Susan headed to the bathroom, remembering that Freddy had insisted that she take the other large bedroom. *"You are the commanding officer, after all,"* he'd said. *The child is kind to a fault. Nearly got him killed twice last year.* She dressed in her jogging outfit and started her stretching "exercises." Half the team would be waiting for her to come out. Today, she had to cut the run to only five miles, with a thirty-minute defensive practice in the middle. Still, she thought that Freddy was coming along well with his self-defense training, and Maggie, his instructor, said that he could take brown in another six months. "Belts! What a farce," Susan muttered. "The training the team gets is for one thing and one thing only, and that isn't play-fighting for trophies. If he is ready for a brown belt, in Maggie's estimation, then the kid could probably take any brown on the face of the earth. In the last attempt on his life, he ducked much faster than we did. However, he still refuses to learn anything except defense. He will not contemplate harming anyone."

"Captain James, the messages are urgent."

"Very well, let's hear the first one."

"'Captain, this is Peters. Your reinforcements are coming in tomorrow at 1:00 p.m. I have cleared your calendar for their arrival. They have been screened, and only eight were removed.' End message."

"Good," Susan said to herself. "That will take the load of security off my back. Our own recruit instructor will oversee things. Well, ladies, expect some real workouts now." Then, to Home, she said, "Acknowledge the first message, and give me the second message, please."

"Good morning, Susan."

"Good morning, Shop. You have a message from Freddy?"

"Yes. Here it is paraphrased: 'Tammy is to be removed from the base and all projects relating to me immediately. Susan, I think Tammy is unconsciously transmitting a craving for her to all men. I believe Tammy transmits all the time, and that without her being present, the men still receive that transmission, even over distance. They're getting irritated because they still feel the craving for her but she's not there to relieve it. Remind Susan that eleven men transferred in with her.' One more thing that Freddy did not add, but I feel it's important—Freddy's love for Becky helped him recognize this problem, and he is very worried about what Becky thinks of him. I feel it would be very good if someone let Becky know that Freddy personally sent Tammy away because of his love for Becky."

"Thank you, Shop."

"You're welcome."

How did Freddy figure that one out when the rest of the specials could not? Susan wondered. Oh well. Love can work wonders, and now that we know Becky is a special, we may have a chance to put the two of them together again. Becky was very angry after Freddy's last visit. "Home, get me Commander Morgan, please."

"Working."

Over the intercom, Susan heard, "Good morning, Captain."

"Good morning, Daphne. Please have Tammy transferred out. Do it within the hour, along with all eleven men who transferred here with her. Then have every man on this base screened and watched for signs of withdrawal from Tammy 'craving.' Freddy says she's transmitting and can't help it. Send her to the special 'kids ranch' in Texas. Give them warning she's coming and why. Please inform her parents, and make sure that Tammy knows that we would be glad to accept her back when she has worked out this problem. I don't want her feelings hurt or her thinking that she is being rejected. Let her know that we're going to help her as much as possible so that she can control this issue and return to us. Transfer the men to someplace remote. They'll need time to get over it."

"Aye aye, Captain. I'll put the team on alert. I think this move could cause some repercussions, especially if anyone finds out that Freddy asked for the transfer. Tammy was very popular with the men. Now we know why."

"You may be right, but with the specials on board the truth will get out anyway. Better we tell everyone the truth and make it look like Freddy saved them again. Especially let it out that it was Freddy's love for Becky that caused him to figure out the problem and immediately send Tammy away."

"That's going to draw some tears from the little girls. They all love Becky. In addition, it may get them back together again. Consider it done, Captain."

"I'm going out now. How many are going with me?"

"Only twenty, Captain."

"Why so few?"

"It's past 6:00 a.m., ma'am."

"Are you saying I'm late, Commander?" Susan asked with a laugh in her voice.

"Yes, ma'am."

"All right. I'm on my way."

That's when it happened. The entire building rocked with the blast.

✦

Gray said, "They are under attack! Now we get to something less boring"

Green said, "Shut up, you fool! Yellows, he is trying something. I feel it, but I do not know what it is."

Gray would have attacked Green, but Blue placed a tentacle on his head and lifted him up. Blue said, "Green, you watch your tone, or I will find another Green to do this reading and allow Gray to have you as his for a full day."

Green nearly turned white with fear.

Big and Little Yellows wrapped me harder, and I temporarily stopped just to let them think they were in control.

Green said, "That is better. Did you catch what he was doing?"

Little Yellows said, "We don't think he actually did anything. He was just testing the control we have on him."

Green ordered, "Double-check the controls on the tank!"

Another Green said, "The tank is working normally, and the indicators show full power."

Blue said, "Green, it is still working, so please continue."

I thought, *Won't they be surprised?*

"Do you know Freddy's abilities toward healing?"

"Yes, ma'am, and he could heal all five, but it would literally kill him."

A little redheaded boy came up and took the girl's hand. "He no do it. He would if haft to; he so nice. But no haft to."

"Who are you, dear?" Susan asked.

"This is my little brother Bobby," Stacy said. "He's able to sense through this shield. Freddy adjusted it so that he could."

"We play game 'gether when he work sometime. I hide; he find. It fun. He say increase my mind shield that way."

"Can you talk to Freddy right now?"

"Yep."

"Please ask him if everything's all right."

"He already tell me. Say not worry. He new toy fix people. Say people be out soonest."

"Captain, this is Shop."

"Shop! It's nice to hear your voice."

"Thank you. Freddy will have me completely connected again in just a few minutes. I'm opening the doors now. Please make room for people to exit. Freddy wants everyone out until you make a complete investigation."

"Tell Freddy that I'm here, and I will start as soon as I can get inside."

"There. That's better."

The doors opened and out came the crew, except Freddy. No one looked harmed. They were all talking about how Freddy saved lives. The captain grabbed one petty officer with torn and bloody clothes and said, "Report."

The petty officer snapped to attention. "The new modification that we made to the laser cannon works better than expected but takes a lot of power, Captain. I think Freddy's original design was better. We blew a generator." With eyes as big as moons, he said, "Captain, I was torn to shreds, and so were several others. I knew I was going to die, but Freddy ran a device over me, and I was completely fine, except for loss of blood. Freddy mumbled and complained that he hasn't worked that part out yet. You know how he gets when he has to use something before he's ready, and it doesn't do everything he wants."

"Petty Officer, you and the others who were hurt are to report to the infirmary," Susan said. She turned to the special girl Stacy. "Please make sure that they don't go back to work until they have a clean bill of health from Dr. O'Brian."

Stacy took hold of the petty officer's arm and said, "This way."

"Young man?" Susan said. "Bobby, is it?"

"Yes, ma'am. You really famous, Cap'n Jam."

"Yes, I'm Captain James. Do you know where Freddy is?"

"He in the top. He look at mess. He know you come him. He berry, berry upset. He say I not be 'fraid of you 'cus you nice person."

Susan smiled and said, "I'll bet he's upset. Thanks." She ran inside after giving orders for a complete investigation.

When Susan reached the tower and the second generator site, there was Freddy. They were high up the cliff and could see the entire home base. *What a beautiful sight*, Susan thought. Yet the small room where the generator was located was blackened and pitted, as if a large bomb had gone off. The waterfall was loud, and Susan realized that although she nearly had to yell to be heard, Freddy's quiet voice was somehow instantly heard, even over all the noise.

"It's a total loss, Susan."

Susan had to agree. "Yes, it is. Why did Shop loose communications? Was she powered by this generator?"

"No, she has her own power source. However, her external communications and some controls were running along that wall." He pointed to a wall that was pitted from the explosion and had bits of metal sticking throughout it. "I had to reroute them through another channel. Luckily, I had a backup set in case I needed a second computer. I haven't needed one, as Shop's been great."

"Thank you, Freddy."

"You deserve a lot of praise, Shop, for the way you calmed people down and for helping me get to the sight of the injured. I'm going to double your abilities after this."

"Thank you."

"You're welcome."

"Do we have a spare generator, Freddy?" Susan asked.

He looked up and said, "No, but I have something new I can put in its place. If they can burn out this generator then I think I need to upgrade anyway." Kicking at it, he added, "This is junk. I'll get it removed and have the new unit set up and running just a few days after we get back. I want to know why the safety circuits didn't trip during an overload. If someone bypassed them, I want that person removed, please."

"Done. Now, Freddy, I'm told you healed five people who were torn up very badly. I can see the loss of blood and some guts on the floor. Want to explain how?"

"No, I don't. Still, you're going to find out anyway, so come this way. There's not much we can do in here right now."

He motioned for Susan to follow him and led her back into the special area reserved just for him. It was supposed to be just a small build area, but Susan could see Freddy had changed things quite a bit. It was nearly as big as the build area they'd just left. He wasn't using much of it, but right in the middle was the longest, sleekest, fastest-looking craft Susan had ever seen. It was beautiful—about a mile long, a quarter-mile wide, and standing easily ten stories.

The hundreds of window lights; smooth, gleaming hall; and sleekness made it look like the fastest vessel ever conceived.

He said, "Stop staring, and come here, please. This is an AutoDoc. Step in, please."

Susan looked skeptical. Freddy was pointing to a large reclining ship's seat, similar to the kind seen in spacecraft. Behind it was a mass of computerized equipment and, in front, two arms. One arm had a scanning device on it, and the other arm had a unit that looked like a fancy laser rifle. He smiled and said, "Come on, Susan. Have I ever let you down?"

"There's always a first time," Susan said.

When she had settled in, Freddy asked, "Comfy?"

"Actually, I am," The couch adjusted itself around her form to perfection, and she felt almost weightless. "Yes. This is great."

He smiled and said, "AD, please analyze the patient. Her title is captain, and her name is Susan James."

A low-level pale green light played over Susan's body, and a baritone voice said, *"Analyzing. Completed. There is nothing major wrong with Captain James. She does have an ulcer. Would you like me to correct the issue?"*

"Please."

Susan felt a slight tingle, and then the AutoDoc said, *"Captain James is now in perfect health."*

"Good. AD, please arrest Captain James."

"Compliance."

"Freddy, thank you for fixing my ulcer, but what are you doing now?"

He held up a picture of Tammy, saying, "I'm going to miss her, aren't you?"

"Tammy? Not really."

"She's so little and frail. I don't think she has any muscle at all. No, she is all softness."

"Yes, she's the perfect picture of a frilly little girl. Now let me go."

"Stop struggling, Tammy." Freddy said.

"Tammy!"

"I really love your small voice; your long, soft hair; and your innocent look."

"Freddy, you're scaring me."

"AD, how long will it take to change the captain here into a perfect replica of my Tammy."

"*Freddy!*" Susan screamed.

"*Three minutes.*"

Freddy nodded. "Please start."

✦

Gray exclaimed, "He is messing with a Black! Is he crazy?"

Green said, "I think these two have some kind of bond. This Tammy has a weapon that can drive their men mad."

Gray said, "They are already mad. We don't need them any madder."

Blue said, "I do not think he is actually harming her. More interesting is the fact that he has a device that can instantly heal."

A voice in the air said, "We want that technology."

All the others except the Yellows went to their knees. I looked and focused on the area where the voice came from, and standing there was a creature of every possible color, which were radiating in ripples. It was nearly translucent but easy to see with my abilities.

I said, "A little late for exchanging technology."

It looked directly at me and seemed surprised that when it moved, I followed. "It sees me. This creature can see me!" It left in a panic.

Little Yellows smiled and said, "Royalty does not like it when someone can see them. It is its most protective ability to be invisible. Without that ability it is vulnerable."

I said, "Oh well. Let him know that our scanners can easily pick him up. Back then, we might not have been able to see through your cloaking device, but we can now."

Little Yellows shuddered. "Perhaps we can come to an understanding."

I said, "Not up to me. I am just an inventor. Would a Red or top scientist have the power to make a treaty?"

Green said, "Of course not. We will continue."

C H A P T E R   4

✦ ✦ ✦

Ꭾᗞ

I smiled as a light blue glow played over the captain's body. She started screaming.

"Freddy! No! *Shop!* Don't do this! Not that little tramp! Every lovesick man on this base will be chasing me! *Stop! Please, no!*" Her pleading went on for only a minute.

I couldn't hold it any longer and just about died laughing. When I could finally get myself together enough to talk, I said, "AD, end the Tammy-tease program. See, Shop? I told you that'd be fun."

"Freddy, I'd run!"

Too late—I was laughing so hard I couldn't move fast enough. Captain James had me and was beating the crap out of my right arm before I knew what was happening.

She laid into me, and I was screaming for her to please stop when Shop said, *"Freddy, some day you're going to have to explain why two minutes of what you consider fun is worth the hours of pain you will endure after she gets through. I will never understand the human person. Oh, that's going to black an eye."*

After what seemed like a long time, Susan picked me up and placed me in the AutoDoc. She stood there looking at me and then said, "AD, arrest Freddy." After a moment, she added, "AD, can you do something to ensure that no damage was done to Freddy during that beating, but do not decrease the pain?"

Darn, she was getting too good at using my equipment.

"I can fix the bruised bone but leave all the weakened muscles. Shop has just asked me to weaken the bladder muscles also. Is this permissible? He will not be able to control his bladder for months."

I tried to get out and said, "AD, cancel that request!"

"I am sorry, but you programmed me not to take orders from the patient. Captain James?"

"Do it, AD. Freddy, I think you're going to enjoy wearing diapers for that childish prank."

The beam started playing over my body.

"Yes, diapers and a little pink baby frock. Sucking on a pacifier and wearing a baby bonnet. Just think how cute you're going to look on TV tonight when we finally put that dome over Luna City."

I screamed, *"No!"* I struggled as much as possible, but my own equipment was keeping me very secure. Finally, the bean stopped, and AD let me go. I got out, crying. The last thing I needed was to be in public view dressed as a baby girl. Yuck!

"You're right, Captain. That was very satisfying."

I asked, "What? Shop, what did you say?"

Susan said, "See how it feels, Freddy, to be teased like that? Now do you understand why I keep telling you not to play jokes on people?"

"Yes, but I can take the joke. It's the beating that hurts."

"Good. Shop, please inform all the team that Freddy just got another beating for pulling a prank on me. Let them know his right arm is very sore."

"Oh, thanks. Every one of them will be looking for reasons to smack my arm."

"You're welcome, Freddy. Now stop with this fun of

yours, or next time I *will* change you into a baby." She waited for my body to calm down and for me to stop rubbing my arm where she concentrated most of her anger. "Let's talk about your new invention."

"The AD is a molecular reorganizer that takes the normal body as a base paradigm and then scans for dissimilarities. If solicited, it takes the divergences and reorganizes the molecules to fit a precise pattern. At the equivalent time, it eliminates any damaged molecules and grows new surrogate molecules through an accelerator that presents a semblance of instantaneous reconditioning."

"Okay, I caught most of that. The team coming out said you repaired them with a small unit. This is fairly big."

I frowned, forgetting that not everyone thinks like I do. I went over to the workbench and picked up the portable. "Susan, this unit is a PAAD—Portable Auxiliary AutoDoctor. It's tied into the computer on the 'fairly big' AD. It gives the doctor using it the ability to quickly scan and fix. The computer to run the AD is large, as it takes quite a bit of memory and programming to make it compatible with all humans. The actual scanner and molecular reorganizing beam can be very small, as you can see. I wanted to do something to help ensure that no one gets killed out there on new planets. I figured that we could put the ADs at the bases, and then the scouting or working teams can take a portable with them. Also, you can put one on each ship and then use the portables for emergencies when the patients can't reach medical facilities."

"Freddy, will this fix all diseases?"

"Should fix anything that puts the body out of normal, and if the unit has previously scanned a person, then it can bring the person back to that state or near to it, if necessary. It cannot correct death, but it can help regeneration of old age or a body-damaging issue, like cancer or spinal damage."

"Freddy, this is great. When can we have this unit?"

I thought out loud, saying, "I need to test it more, but after that it should be ready. I'd guess in about a year."

"Why so long?"

Her question upset me, and I wondered if she could see it in my expression. It was such a silly question. I said in a rather matter-of-fact tone, "I have work to do. This"—I pointed to the AD—"was just a fun side project." I pointed to the new ship. "That's my new toy."

"What type ship is it?"

"Not ready to say yet, but it's going to be really fun."

"Can I get a tour?"

"Not yet. I have a lot of work to do on the design and at this time, it's rather dangerous."

"How long will it take you to complete this ship?"

"Another year at this rate. I have other things to do, you know. Schedules are getting busy again."

"How long would it take to complete the AD and PAAD if you concentrated on them?"

I had to think about that. "A week at most, Susan. Two weeks to complete the paperwork and any fixes before patenting. Why?"

"If I clear your schedule for, say, six months, could you finish the AD first and then finish your ship?"

"Yes. I could do that. Why?"

"Freddy, this AD"—she patted the unit—"has a lot of potential. Every hospital and most homes will want an AutoDoc, as will schools, major businesses, fire departments, and every ambulance. This could cut the cost of medical care down to a reasonable level, here and everywhere. Freddy, this could be considered your most important invention yet."

"Won't the president be mad at me if we put this out?"

"What? Why?"

"She's worried about the population issue. This would

increase that issue a lot. That's why I only considered it for the bases and ships. If we let this out to the general populace, then they will live longer, and the only way to die early would be in a fatal accident. Also, you can change your appearance with it, including your fingerprints and retinas."

"Amazing." She sat in thought for a minute and then said, "You're correct, but it will take several years to get that many built and out there to the public. By then, we'll be colonizing other planets. Besides, with the help of our new scanners we can identify people no matter how they've changed themselves—unless they can change their mental patterns and DNA."

"Oh, this won't allow changes to mental patterns or DNA, but it does do birth control."

"Birth control?"

"Sure. The unit is programmed to make you incapable of having children, if requested, and reversing the effects whenever you want. I made it possible to simply not have children unless you actively want to have them. It can clean arteries so bypass surgery is no longer necessary. A complete physical with repair of any issues will take approximately five minutes, and that includes a print-out of the results."

"Freddy, this is great. Please work to finish this project first."

"Very well, but I'm going to need someone else to do the mass building and design. And my space program comes first. I want priority on all units coming off the line."

"I'll have it set up. Same company that's making your computer units now?"

"Yes, they'll be good for the computer system, but I think we need someone else for the seat and for the scanning and repairing equipment. The last company started going downhill on quality."

"I'll give them warning and one more try."

"No. Please find someone better and more honest. I want it commonly known that if vendors don't keep quality at 100 percent then we will drop them. No excuses; no second chances. The people on my ships won't have a chance if something fails in space. I won't have people dying because some company skimped on quality. If it means we start building the equipment ourselves, then so be it."

✦

Little Yellows said to me, "We wish our ships were built that way. You would not believe the problems we have."

I said, "I already know."

Yellows took a better hold, and Green didn't even notice the exchange.

✦

Susan said, "I know the issues. I'll take care of everything. You finish this project so we can patent it. Freddy, you're a pest sometimes, and I will be angry at you for a long time for that prank. I'll probably have nightmares. I can't think of anything worse than turning into a sweet little frilly girl like Tammy. At the same time, I love you for the things you do for others." She gave me a hug and kissed my forehead, but as she was leaving she swatted my right arm.

"Ouch!" I healed myself and went back to work.

It wasn't long before Shop reminded me that I needed to prep for going to Luna. So I got up and left for home.

I went to my room and stripped out of my dirty jumper, took a shower, and combed my hair. It's down below my waist and causes me all kinds of problems, like choking me when I sleep and getting in my mouth when I eat. If my hair didn't store energy in the protein I can use for healing, I'd cut it all off. At least I don't have problems with tangling or split ends. Using my healing talent, I keep my hair straight and healthy. Laid out on my bed was a new jumper, so I picked it up. Whoever dropped it off picked up my old one for cleaning. This one was dark blue with a bright white collar and about half an inch of white on the ends of the short sleeves. On the left pocket was a four-inch embroidered insignia of home base, complete with waterfalls. Looking closely, I realized how intricate the insignia is. On the right collar was an embroidered insignia that looked like a golden eye. The golden eye indicates that I'm a "special." Yuck. The last thing I need to do is advertise that I can read minds. On the left collar was another insignia that looked like a planet with a long, thin ship crossing in front of it, with two tiny letters underneath: ES. The last time they did this to me, they used pins to attach the insignias. I took them off and refused to put them back on. I remember the argument like it was yesterday ...

"Captain," I said, "I am not in the military, and I do not need any rank."

"Freddy, you're the boss of this gang, and people need to understand that you're who you are."

"Okay, then, I'll wear a name tag." I stomped off.

Now I had a name tag, all right. It was embroidered over my left pocket in gold. I really don't mind all the decorations, but they snuck in six gold stars in a circle around the letters ES. This says that everyone has to salute me. It makes me equal to an admiral!

I went to the closet and dug around for something else to wear. Everything had the emblems. How embarrassing this was going to be. I had to put the dome on Luna, and I was stuck with these stupid badges. I tucked the collar inside the jumper and finished getting dressed. As I walked down the stairs, Colleen stopped me, and she untucked my collar.

"Freddy, you leave that out. We have a lot of new personnel, and there are a lot of children on the base. It's hard enough identifying people without you trying to hide who you are."

"Ah, come on, Colleen. They can still see my name tag."

"Not good enough. We have three Freddys at the base, and one is about your age. He had everyone saluting him and giving him anything he wanted until he tried that with Personnelman Second Class Dorothy Pendelson. She nearly had him shot when she yelled, 'Imposter!' So, no way. You wear that collar on the outside, young man."

"Yes, ma'am." I resolved to tuck it back in as soon as she was out of sight, but every time I did, someone was there to untuck it. Everyone, even the other specials, were in on the game. Several of the youngest ones even followed me. Every military person we passed snapped to attention and saluted—most with amusement written all over their faces. This was going to be a long day.

✦

Blue asked, "Does every one of these humans dislike having high rank? Is it some sort of stigma to be above someone else?"

Gray said, "We have seen that their higher-ranking officers demand obedience. They enjoy the privileges of rank almost like we do."

Big Yellows said, "The politicians have a ranking system that is nearly like ours, and they follow those ranks closely and try to become higher in rank."

Green said, "Our own scientists are ranked on abilities. Many do not like having rank, as it means that they have to spend time away from their projects to handle people and nonscientific work. The higher the rank, the less time you have to invent. This is a Red. He wants to invent."

Gray said, "He is very good at it."

Green said with a smile, "Yes, he is. But if he had more rank, would he not have more noninventing to do?"

Blue said, "Ask him."

Green said, "I know you hear the conversation. Why do you hate having rank?"

I said to all of them, "Even with the highest rank, I would not have to work at anything besides inventing. Captain James ensures that. If I did, I would stop and go someplace else to invent. The reason I do not like rank is that I do not like to tell others what to do, and I don't want them expecting me to lead them. It is a great responsibility and power that belongs to the politicians or Blues. In this, we are the same as you. The higher up we become in our ranking, the more power we have, and we are looked at as the politicians of the group. I don't want that responsibility. I am not good at it, and I don't want that kind of power. Now, I have a question for you."

Blue said, "What is that question?"

"You think you are superior to us. Then explain to me why we outgrew the stage of greed and domination in which you are still stuck."

Gray yelled angrily, "We are not greedy and do not dominate for the fun of it!" Oh my, that did not go over well.

Green said, "If you look at it from a scientific point of view, as this Red does, then yes, we are and do."

Blue said, "I would not call us greedy."

Yellows asked, "Then what do you call stealing planets from other species when we do not really need them?"

Black walked into the room. Black was a big alien that moved in such a way as to be hard to see until it stopped—and then it looked powerful and almost magical, as it phased in and out of reality. It said, "I call it destroying the enemy before it knows we are there. The human race has been highly aggressive until lately. It is our belief that they would eventually become the power in this sector of the galaxy. We talked long and hard about what we should do. Many wanted us to wait and see. Others wanted complete annihilation immediately. We compromised. We were going to try to make you warrior slaves."

I said, "If you know anything about our history, you would know that would fail. Even if you succeeded, you would fail. We may be caught and enslaved, but we will never be slaves. We would find a way to become free."

Black said, "We are beginning to realize this, and that brings us back to total destruction. Green, what is the purpose of continuing with this research?"

Green said, "We are trying to find out all possible information on this species and what they are capable of. This one knows exactly that."

Black said, "I doubt it will tell us much, and we will learn little if this ship is blown to bits. We need to give him back or kill him, and do it soon. Continue, but make it quick."

CHAPTER 5

✦ ✦ ✦

SLOPPY WORK

It was going to be a day to remember in more ways than one. If everything worked, then we'd be flying my new moving ship down to Southern California to pick up the moon dome. The old moving ship could not safely move it. The dome was too big and cumbersome. Weight is not a problem by itself, but size and weight distribution is an issue, especially when you're still in the atmosphere. First, we have to get the ship out of the mountain. The ship is wider than the hangar bay doors by seventy feet and at least twenty-three feet too tall. Everyone says it will never fit.

For a while, people were discouraged about working on it, as they thought that I was making a big mistake. They even christened the ship the ES *Freddy's Folly*. I tried to point out that I would not make a ship that I could not use, but only the SEAL team believed me—and not all of them. About eight weeks ago I made an inspection of the latest assemblies. After seeing how badly the work had been done, I became seriously mad and kicked everyone out and off the project. During the inspection I discovered potentially deadly mistakes. When I asked why, the answer I received was, "We'll fix it." But the feelings I received were, "*It'll never fly anyway."* Susan talked me into letting them come back to work, but I had a talk with them first. Susan had them assembled in the yard; I can remember it quite clearly.

We were standing up on a platform looking down on a crowd of people. Susan tried to get them to quiet down, but nothing happened. They were just too excited. She motioned for the lieutenant to bring things to order. Lt. Jacquelyn Uniceson, limited duty officer, was the master chief when all this started, and she could control anything or anyone. The moment she gave a hand signal, shots were fired from several places. It became deadly quiet after that. The lieutenant gave orders in a loud, booming voice, "Anyone else talks out of turn, shoot them." Of course they wouldn't, as the lieutenant had her hand in a signal that said she was kidding, but the civilians didn't know this.

Capt. Susan James stepped up to the podium and addressed the assembly. "I have a few words before I turn this over to Freddy. The reason for this assembly is that Freddy is upset with the work some of you are doing. He has informed me that the shoddy work on his latest ship will result in deaths and possibly will destroy the entire ship and everyone on it. He has let me know that the reason for this poor work is because some of you believe that Freddy will never be able to get the ship out of the mountain. Just to let you know, Freddy says it's no problem. Here's some information for you: people thought that going to Mars was impossible; Freddy did it. People thought that traveling faster than light was impossible; Freddy did that too. Freddy has invented over one thousand new and "impossible" things that the world now uses. New energy sources, new vehicles, new computers, the scanners, the shields." She opened her arms wide. "He built this home from a toxic trash heap, and he built the ES *Protectress* and saved the world. I don't understand why you don't believe him. The other specials say he's telling the truth when he says that it's no problem. And now he says you're doing poor work in building his newest ship, so he has something to say to you." She stepped down from the podium.

I took the stand and said, "Everyone who is working on my building-moving ship will be going on the trip with us. If I'm going to die because you didn't do the best job you can, then you're going to die with me. Understand: this ship may be used in the war between the Menseains and the Sycloyeds and needs to be top of the line. I hear most of you talking about the war nearly every day. I am trying to help plan for that possibility. Don't slow me down, please." I stepped down and left.

Susan, taking her time so that my words could sink in, slowly walked back to the podium and said, "No one leaves this base until that ship's ready. Everyone working on the project will be going into space, no excuses. That's the order. I would suggest that you check your work very carefully and then check each other's work. Freddy told me that he will not check it and that he expects a full and complete test run out past Pluto and on time. Lieutenant, please dismiss everyone."

I was back in the house before they were dismissed, so I didn't see, but I was told that nearly everyone ran to the shop and started working on the ship. Of course, I did have the shop companion, an invisible portable scanner controlled by the shop computer, check every bit of work over the next few weeks and all the previous work. Most mistakes had been corrected, though it took a lot of very long days and nights for many people. I found a few things and mind-touched the needed people to make them worried and recheck those spots. They did, and now all is looking very good, I hope.

Now the ship was ready to go. I'd gone back to my room to hide from the saluting, but now it was time to eat, so I headed down to lunch. Only the main house residents and a few honored guests eat in the dining room now; it used to be everyone. Small groups are so much easier to handle. I sat down at the wall side in the middle of the table. Susan once offered me the head, but I find it easier to talk to people if I'm not the one they think is in charge. Besides, I'm not in charge. The head of the table would just give a wrong impression, and the specials would see right through it. As I was sitting down, I noticed that Tammy was gone, along with two of the men who always seemed to be around her. In their places were three others.

Nicole Nickelson was on the right. She is a special, a clairvoyant who has the ability to sense danger and other things about a minute before everyone else does. Doesn't sound like much, but it was her warning that caused me to quicken my steps when a young girl about my age tried to get through the crowd last year. It would have been very embarrassing, getting a hug and kiss from her right on television and in front of thousands. Later, the young girl was brought up to see me at the hotel.

We talked, and I found out the silliest thing. She is Julia Pears, and I have a fan club. Can you believe it? This girl was the president of the Freddy Anderson Fan Club. My goodness, I must have turned eight shades of red. The teasing that I received over that—and still get—could make me a hermit. The team stopped teasing me after a few months, and they put a stop to most others, but every now and then I get letters from them. Apparently, the captain has hired someone to write back to my fan club and say nice things. Why am I prattling on about this? Because the one in the center of the three new people was Julia Pears. Julia is a very lovely, redheaded, extremely frilly girl about my age. She is skinny, lacking muscle but healthy, with a good, organized mind. She wore a pink dress with lots of lace and ruffles. Her naturally green eyes sparkle whenever she is about to embarrass me. I wanted to ask, "Who let you in here?" Instead, I said, "Hi. Nice to see you again."

She looked me right in the eye and said with a smile, "I can see by the dark red you turned when you saw me that what I've been hearing is true. We don't really care that you don't think you deserve a fan club. It's one of the things we love about you. You're stuck with us, though, and we all love you—all eighty-three thousand of us."

My eyes must have nearly popped out of their sockets, and I stopped breathing. Katie, who was sitting on my right, slapped me on the back, saying, "Breathe." I did after she hit me several more times. I got up to leave.

Susan asked, "Freddy, what are you doing?"

Not taking my eyes off Julia, I said, "I'm going to the shop. I'll see you in a few weeks."

"Sit down, Freddy." I didn't move, so she said, "*Sit!*" I sat back down. Susan turned to Julia. "Young lady, if you ever do something like that again, I will stop inviting you to this base or anywhere else we may be. Do you understand?"

With a pout, Julia said, "Yes, ma'am, but I do want to point out that Freddy has not been answering our letters. Someone else has, or he would know how many people are in his fan club. I expected as much, and that's why I told him."

Susan said, "Julia, you must understand that Freddy gets over ten thousand letters a month. Some of the letters are from pranksters and some from honest people who want something. He is so kind that he would probably give away everything he has to help people, and then we would not have the benefit of his inventions. We've hired several people who think a lot like Freddy to answer for him. It was one of those who invited you after getting my approval. I invited you so that Freddy can spend a little more time learning about his fan club. He has no idea. He has no time for answering fan mail, and the world cannot afford to waste his time on these issues. If you hadn't noticed, the mail is signed Office of Freddy. If you get one with his signature or mine, then you will know we personally answered it."

I looked at Susan and said, "I had no idea. You're right, of course. If I had to answer even a small portion of that much mail, I would have never invented the carrier, and the AD might have never gotten off the drawing board."

"That's right, Freddy. There is almost no hate mail anymore, although one letter bothers me. It's about experimenting on specials, and they wanted samples of your blood. We will talk about that later. Most of the mail asks for help with something, selling something, or wanting something. We sort through it and pull out the important mail, and then it goes through a process that cuts it down to two categories: business and private. You receive over three hundred bills, invoices, or communications for parts or materials that you've ordered." She leaned forward. "It's how we know you're working on that new ship. That's business mail, and we take care of it. The private mail is from almost everyone possible. You've received a letter from the Vatican, several presidents and other high officials, many congressmen and senators, and hundreds of girls who want you to come to their parties, There's a lot about the war between the Menseains and the Sycloyeds. We toss most of them out and answer only those we deem important."

I thought a moment and then turned to Julia and said, "I just can't take the time to answer the mail, Julia, but I will answer three pieces personally each month. Susan, I'm sure you come across some letters that you think would be good for me to answer."

"Yes, we do, but we don't want to slow you down."

"I think I can answer three a month. I can dictate to

Home or Shop and then print them out and sign them. I have a lot of busy work that takes no real thought. Shop or Home could read them to me, and I could answer them. Three is not too many, and one a month from my favorite fan, Julia." I looked at her and quickly said, "Just so I don't get blindsided again. All the rest of the fans can send letters to her. She can write to me after compiling all the needed information." I smiled at her and added, "As president, I'm sure you don't mind answering thousands of letters a month, do you?" I didn't give her time to answer. I saw her jaw drop and knew she was about to become defensive. I then said, "And two others that your team deems proper. Would that be okay, Susan?"

"Yes, Freddy. We'll try that but no more. We'll forward all fan mail to Julia, then. First thing: the world needs that AD completed. I think it takes priority over anything else, and I want to read the letters you send out before you send them. We need to know what you're promising people."

"Sure, you can read them, and then someone can mail them for me. I really don't understand your obsession with my AD, Susan. The world doesn't have it now, so why is it so important to get it going right this minute?"

✦

Blue said, "He's joking, right?"

Green said, "He's a Red. Just like ours, he doesn't see all the possibilities, just the ones he is aiming to fix."

I added, "Again, that's another color's responsibility. I invent, and they figure out the uses."

Yellows said, "It is the same with us. Now be quiet, please."

✦

Susan turned to the third new person. "Freddy has something that he would like to tell you." She turned back to me and said, "Please tell Alice about your AD."

I shrugged and then had Shop pull it up on the screen, and I told her all about it. The whole table was silent, and Alice was crying. I looked at Susan and said, "What's the matter? What'd I do?"

Alice got up, came around the table, and hugged me. She was crying and thanking me over and over.

When she was finally pulled off me and made to sit back down, Susan said, "Alice has lost three children to sudden infant death syndrome. She sent us a letter, begging us to let her talk to you. You're the top special in healing. You have the best ability, and she begged us to get your help to save her fourth child."

Alice asked through tears, "Your AutoDoctor—can it analyze what's wrong with her and fix her?"

I thought for a second and said, "Yes, it can. Where is your baby now?"

"In the living room."

I got up and went to the living room. Two of the team were watching a man sitting with a child under monitors that looked a lot like a modification of my scanning equipment. I walked up to him. "You're the father?"

"Yes."

I ran my hand over the equipment. "Susan, is this how my equipment is being used?"

"Yes. This is your equipment. We sell to the hospitals for medical use at a much-reduced price so they can afford it. Your scanners have replaced a lot of other types of equipment."

I went over to her and hugged her, saying, "Thank you." Then I walked over to the baby and gently picked her up. "Have the doctors and other specials seen her?"

"Yes, but they could not find anything."

"Have Stacy Michaels report here immediately, please." The captain made a quick hand signal, and a girl ran out.

It took only a minute for Stacy to show up. A precog (person with precognition) told her, and she was already on the way. When she reached the house and saw me in the living room, she said, "I've already checked her, Freddy. I can't find anything."

"Then let's check her together. I'll show you how." She placed her right hand on the one I had on the child's forehead and one hand on my arm, where we touched skin to skin. I closed my eyes and looked at the child. I could feel Stacy's astonishment at what I was doing. I was looking at each individual molecule. I found nothing, so I looked at the baby's mind. I found nothing. Then I looked at the chemicals in her body and found the problem. She was being poisoned— not enough to detect normally, but it was highly toxic. It wasn't food causing the problem either. It was a chemical that was modified in the brain. I traced the path and found an abnormality in the medulla oblongata section of the brain stem. I changed it to what I knew was normal, and the poison started to diminish. The chemical started changing correctly to a protein that helps brain development. It would take a few days, but her body would now correct itself. I opened my eyes and asked, "Did you catch that?"

Stacy said in wide-eyed awe, "I caught every bit of it."

"Can you duplicate what I did?"

"Yes, not as well as you did, but with practice I could. I never realized I could see that way. It's so much more efficient. It saves power, and I could find and correct many more diseases using that method."

I smiled at her. "You practice, then. You have the power to heal far better than I can. Exercise your talent." I looked down at the baby and kissed her on the cheek. I passed her back to the father, letting him know what the problem was, that it was fixed, and that the poison would be completely out of the body in just a couple of days. "Watch her very closely for the next week, but I don't think you'll have any more problems after the poison is gone." I received more hugs from the mother and a big handshake and thank-you from the father. They stayed in the living room under guard, and we returned to the dining room table.

Susan asked me, "How did you feel about your scanning equipment being used for the care of the sick, Freddy?"

"Very good. I like that. I like it a lot."

She smiled and so did the others, including Julia. Susan then said, "How did you feel about saving that child's life?"

"That I loved doing."

"And how did you feel helping the parents?"

"I loved that also."

"Your AD will do that same thing for thousands every day for the rest of your life and all eternity."

I stared at her for a few minutes with wide eyes and said, "I'll get on it right after I get the dome in place. I'll need Stacy's and Dr. O'Brian's help."

"You'll have it. Stacy is still underage, so she has to volunteer and get permission, but I don't think they'll be a problem. Let's eat before it gets cold."

Blue said, "He cares a lot about his people not being hurt."

Gray said, "We can use that." The others looked at him as if he'd profaned.

Little Yellows said, "It's not just his people. He cares about our people also. He does not like to see anything harmed."

Blue said, "You know the Fimireians. Kindhearted to the last. Would never harm anyone or anything intentionally. But they fought like Rapggersins when we tried to invade."

Gray said, "It was a grand fight. Many heroes on both sides."

Blue looked like he wanted to hit the Gray and said, "We lost eighty-six ships and ten thousand men to that one battle, and we could have achieved the same results by asking first. They were friendly!"

Gray said somewhat proudly, "Now they're gone. They will not present a problem anymore."

Big Yellows said, "Yes, now they are gone, so we do not have the benefit of their knowledge, their culture, their friendship, and their help in our main two wars. They would have been great allies."

Blue said, "Their books tell us they did not like the undead."

I said, "Who does?"

All stared at me as if I'd just grown wings. Blue asked, "You helped a ghost. Yet you say you do not like undead?"

I said, "First, ghosts are not undead. They are the dead not at rest. And in that situation I helped the ghosts to give them rest so they would stop haunting the town. They tend to leave permanently if they are at rest, though it is said that this war may cause our dead to rise and take vengeance. As I've said, we never give up. Not even in death." For the first time I felt fear from all of them, and it was because of me. They fear ghosts and possibly the undead. I added, "I need to know something."

Blue asked, "What do you need to know, little one?"

"Are these undead creatures heading our way?"

Blue answered, "If we cannot stop them, they will take over this entire galaxy."

I said nothing else but Yellows could sense my emotions

and read what I was transmitting to our fleet about the undead. I sent: *"According to their thoughts, they are in two other major wars. They are in a war against undead on one front and intelligent machines on another. Check their files. Find out if this is correct. They may be lying to me. If it is correct, after destroying them, I have an idea on how to fight the undead. Actually, I have several. I cannot speak now, as they are monitoring. Check my second book on extra-dimensional travel and my twenty-eighth and six hundred fourth note on the ethereal."*

Little Yellows said, "This creature just warned his fleet about the undead. He has given them clues on making some kind of weapon against the undead and against ethereal creatures. In perfect knowledge, as if it were a fact, he told them that after destroying us, he has several ideas on how to fight the undead."

Gray frowned. "These pathetic creatures cannot destroy us. Did you catch what the weapon was?"

Yellows answered, "No, only that it would be very useful. Are we correct in believing we still have not found a way to destroy the undead?"

Gray said, "We are holding them in place by destroying their ships, but we cannot destroy the creatures themselves."

Yellows said, "This one can."

Green said, "Lets continue. Maybe we can find a clue."

CHAPTER 6

✦ ✦ ✦

DOING THE IMPOSSIBLE

We sat down and had a very good lunch of spaghetti and tiny meatballs that were very flavorful. The president came in with several of her approved special-service guards, and we exchanged hugs. The issue came up several times and in different ways about how I was going to get the ship outside. I just smiled and continued eating.

Susan said, "He likes his surprises. He's not allowed to tease"—she paused and gave me a very harsh look—"anymore. So he gets his kicks in other ways. All children"—this time she smiled at me—"need a fun outlet."

"Captain, you're not going to get me mad at you with that 'children' remark, and I'm not going to be teased into giving away how I'm going to do this. After all, I am just a child," I said in a meek voice. "I still have babysitters. I'm afraid that when you see how easy it is to accomplish, it will be anticlimactic. Everyone will go away saying, 'How simple.'"

Just about the time we were finishing up the last of the

garlic bread, someone asked. "Are we going to have time to brush our teeth?"

I stopped eating after that and went upstairs to ensure that the media would not report that I had bad breath. I took the time to comb my hair again. Several months ago, I'd told Susan that I needed a haircut or at least a trim, but she talked me out of it. Something about my long hair being my status symbol. I went outside and couldn't believe how many people were waiting to see how I was going to accomplish getting the ship outside. The area I was sending it to was clear, though the ship would take up a lot of room over several raised parklike sections. It would hover over that area until the landing gear found the ground and then level itself. Everyone on the base must have been there.

The team had emptied the area that I'd requested for landing the craft. The reporters were set up and ready. I went inside the shop and entered my private area.

"Good afternoon, Shop."

"Hi, Freddy."

"We're going to test our new system today."

"Which one?"

"The TP, of course. We'll be moving the Folly out into the yard. Is everyone outside?"

"Yes. I have looked over your math, Freddy. I must say, I don't understand it."

"We'll work on that. I need you to understand it so that you can watch for mistakes. Where's the issue?"

"I don't think I have a processor capable of handling that complicated level of physics."

"That's not good. You have the fastest, most powerful processor in the world. I'll work on it later. Please make it one of my top priorities."

"It's on the list as number three, Freddy. Number one is now the AutoDoc."

"Good. Let's get this show on the road before everyone becomes nervous. Scan the yard, and ensure that no one moves into the landing area."

"*Scanning. All clear at this time.*"

"Good." I turned to my console and started up the equipment. I scanned the ship and locked it in and then scanned the area to where I wanted the ship to move. "Shop, remodulate shields at coordinates 15.2.28 on the base grid."

"*Shield remodulated to allow for transference through the ethereal.*"

"Thank you." I hit the button and teleported the ship to that spot.

✦

Gray yelled, "*What?*"

Blue said, "Quiet! Green, continue."

✦

Some people look at teleportation—or as some people call it, transmitting—as one of two possibilities. First is the copy or faxing method, where you completely scan an object, send the information details across space, and reconstruct the object from materials on hand in the desired place.

This theory is nice but impractical. For instance, if I were to teleport you outside of my building, where am I going to get the exact parts and materials to build an exact copy of you, how would I copy your exact thoughts or emotions into your new body? What if the transmission of the information about you gets distorted? Nothing we have, to date, can transmit pure information, distortion-free. Just the tiniest glitch in information transfer would be devastating, and you would be dead, if you're lucky. And what happens to the original? Either the original is destroyed, or now there are two of you. I wasn't happy about either of those possibilities.

The second is called "breakdown and reassemble." This is where you change the molecular structure of an object so that the parts can be easily transferred and then reassembled somewhere else. However, you still have to transfer the parts to the other place. Say you can put the parts onto a laser beam. Great—now you're stuck with line of sight, and anything that disrupts the beam would destroy the object. Also, you had better hope that nothing disrupts the beam. Anything from a dust speck to a planet can interfere, and radiation or solar winds or other transmissions can interfere. Even a cricket that makes its leg-rubbing noise can create sound waves that can interfere and change the information transfer. Very dangerous way to move objects, and I would never move something alive by using that method.

My teleportation system does not break down anything. It does not copy and does not fax. As I could teleport myself from one place to another, I became curious as to how. A little research led me to believe there were other planes of existence, and I was crossing them. I researched this and I found the astral plane. This plane occupies the same space as ours, but objects on the astral plane are not affected by most objects on the prime material plane (our normal plane). In fact, the only thing that crosses both planes is energy, or force. This gave me an idea. If I could move an object into the astral plane and then use force to control where it moves, then I could move objects through walls. It took a lot of work to develop a way to move objects into the astral plane, but one day I did it. I lost that object. I tried over and over until I figured out that I was moving them too far. One inch on the astral plane is hundreds of miles on the prime material plane. After that, it was just a matter of breaking down the distance variables and walls. I could move a glass of water from one table to another without spilling a drop, even with walls and other objects in the way.

Now, when I teleport myself it's by using pure thought, and the astral plane kicks me out at the desired position. I wasn't going to make objects think, so I would have to rely on the dots. Everyone receives a dot when they enter my workshop, as the dots watch, report, and provide communication. My dots are small balls of pure force that hover near the left ear. I created and sent one dot with each object and had it move the desired distance. Now I had control over my transmitter system, which could teleport objects anywhere in the world.

"Shop, please scan for the Folly."

"The Folly has teleported to the landing area and is completely intact."

I jumped up, shouting, *"Yes!"* I knew it would work. All the little moving around of things and the practice had paid off. "Shop, please give me a view of the yard and the Captain's face."

"Compliance."

There she was, her mouth open so far that her chin was almost hitting her chest. She was in total shock, and it was wonderful. All that security had paid off. This was even better than pretending to turn her into Tammy. She couldn't punish me for doing this, but she was going to try to get the information out of me. I shut down the transmitter and waited a few minutes so that people had time to calm down, and the lieutenant had time to restore order. It was a madhouse out there. When everything was pretty much ready, I left my area and headed out. Both guards congratulated me on my accomplishment, and I thanked them. As soon as I exited the main door, the cheering started again. I was put up on the shoulders of two team members and carried over to the captain and the media. After they put me down on the raised platform and after I received handshakes and hugs from almost everyone, I held up my hand for quiet. I had the biggest smile on my face. I was so happy. If it hadn't worked, then this would have been completely different. When everyone calmed down and there was quiet, I stepped up to the microphones.

"I know this is the wrong thing to do, and it's slightly childish," I said. "But as the captain so elegantly pointed out during lunch, I am just a child. This is for all the people who thought I couldn't do it, for the people who helped me name this ship *Freddy's Folly*." With a laugh in my voice, I said, *"I told you so!"*

The cheers roared throughout the canyon. I couldn't help but think that this was definitely one of the best days of my life.

Susan said, "Time to climb aboard."

We went down the ramp and then up into the ship. We were followed by several people from the team, the crew that was picked to run the ship, the media, our president, and all the people who had worked on the ship. There were over two hundred people in all. The crew started her up. Testing was completed, and we were flying past Pluto in less than three hours. Each person who worked on building her stayed with the crew person who ran the part of the ship they worked on. We found out later that this was an excellent eye-opener for the workers, and it generated a lot of feedback for improvements. When the flying tests were over, I could feel the jubilation from the crew, the workers, and the team. I turned to Susan and the media.

"Well, Susan, the primary test of my transmitter system worked well. I was worried that teleportation might adversely affect parts of the ship, but it looks like everything is doing great. The ship's crew and the workers did a wonderful job.

I'm very proud of them. I would say we're ready to test the rest of the ship. We can pick up the dome now."

Susan looked at the ship's captain and said, "Captain Nervloe, Freddy is extremely happy with the way the crew and the workers have pulled together and completed this ship and the current testing. He would like to thank you, the crew, and the workers for the great effort it took to get this ship on line and within time. Please let everyone know he gives his highest respect and has great pride in their accomplishments. He gives his permission to keep everyone onboard for the next step. Please proceed."

I turned to the media and said, "She does that really well. Much better than I could."

They smiled, and all started talking quietly into their mikes.

Susan was smiling also. "Freddy?"

"Yes."

"How long have you had a working transmitter for teleportation?"

"Oh, I've had the transmitter fully functional for about a week now, but it's got a long way to go before I can release it. The first ship with it will be the—" I stopped and put my mental shields up fully. I smiled at her and waved my finger at her, as if she were a naughty little girl. "No reason to talk about that now," I added.

"Only a week? Then how were you going to get it out before that?"

I reached over and whispered in her ear, "I have no idea." We were interrupted by engineering, but I could see that Susan was not going to leave it at that.

✦

Gray said, "Teleportation! He can travel into and out of the astral and possibly the ethereal! Is he royalty?"

Green said, "No. Apparently only a select few have the ability, and he is the strongest."

Blue said, "Teleporting himself is one thing but an entire ship? That is another technology we need. Complete annihilation of this species is not acceptable at this time."

Little Yellows was near to tears. "We would think not. Their reinforcements are coming."

Gray said, "Do not worry, Yellows. We are ready and will smash his fleet, and when our reinforcements arrive, we will smash what is left."

CHAPTER 7

✦ ✦ ✦

BRINGING
IT HOME

"Captain Nervloe, this is engineering."

"Go ahead, Lieutenant."

"Captain, we have a special panel down here that is not part of the training. The workers said that Freddy installed it himself. I don't know what it's for, but it just lit up and appears very active."

"Hold on."

The captain turned to me. "Freddy?"

"Yes, sir?" I said, feeling kind of guilty.

"Did you install some new equipment down in engineering?"

"Yes, sir."

"It's all lit up and active. What's it for?"

My face must have turned red, as his eyebrows rose ever so slightly, but his mind was saying, *"I hope the kid didn't do something rash."*

"Captain, may I, please?" I motioned to the science station.

"Be my guest."

I went over to the station and started working on the issue. I talked as I was working. "This new system is an energy-warning unit. It detects energy fluctuations of unknown origins, like radiation, electromagnetic emissions from stars and black holes, explosions, and extreme solar winds that could be a hazard to navigation. The problem is that I haven't programmed it for what is or is not normal yet. I thought I left it turned off."

"You did," said someone from engineering. "We activated it when we did start up."

"Lieutenant, just a suggestion," I said. "Don't power up something without checking first. I left a note on that unit, saying not to touch it."

"Understood, Freddy."

"Captain, the energy emissions are from somewhere out in space. I'm coordinating with scanners for a fix. Just a couple more seconds—there." I turned to the main screen. There were three ships—two big ships shaped like smooth black cylinders at least eight hundred meters in diameter, with no lights or emissions, were chasing a small vessel that resembled a dolphin with one large eye in the center. The small one was shielded. I touched a few more buttons, and the ships were identified and notations placed on the screen. The small ship was one of our friends. We knew that they called themselves the Menseains. The two larger ships belonged to the Sycloyeds. The Menseains were at war with the Sycloyeds and apparently so was half our sector of the galaxy.

The Menseains are a benevolent race that believes in helping other races, like us humans. They had proven that they were capable of living on the same planet with us without causing issues. They had been watching us for thousands of years, and the information we downloaded last year gave as an understanding of how many times they had saved the human race from near disasters. Theologians and historians are—and for many years will be—studying that information. That download also gave us a lot of information on the other side of this conflict, and we knew that the creatures in the bigger ships would someday come our way. They are insectoid in nature, but nothing we ever imagined.

The Sycloyeds have only six legs and stand about two feet tall, or four feet tall when on their back four legs. According to the information we obtained, they look almost like a fly. In fact, they do fly.

The captain took over quickly. He contacted the fleet and let them know what was going on. The fleet mobilized instantly, sending our closest ships—two shark-class defenders to meet the two Sycloyed ships and destroy them and then bring in the Menseain, if he needed help.

We were at San Diego, picking up the dome, but the talk was on the conflict. Ever since we found out about the war between the Menseains and the Sycloyeds, people have been screaming that the government should do something. There is a big fear in the human race about certain things. The undead, mostly because of movies, are at the top of the list and then insects and intelligent machines. Insects were high enough that 93 percent of the people surveyed around the world said that we should consider them for total annihilation. The rest said we should, at the minimum, help our friends. The governments around the world followed the views of the populace but suggested that we not join in the war without being invited. Besides, our ships were not tested against an enemy that could shoot back.

That was bunk, and they knew it. I built my ships to protect, and they could easily help. Since I gave them the shield technology over a year ago, contact with the Menseains had been zero. We sent out probes to watch, and reports said that our friends were not doing very well. Still, the president refused to get involved without an invitation. I tried to send out ships myself, but Susan stopped me.

"Let the higher-ups make war decisions, Freddy," she said. "You don't want to go down that road."

She was right, of course. Still, it's difficult to sit by when someone you like is getting pounded. However, now we might have the chance to hear firsthand how things are going.

Picking up the dome turned out to be really simple and somewhat boring. Though it was over fifty miles in diameter, the tractor beams on this ship easily handled it. As the captain was playing the video feed around the ship, most people were around the ship's screens, watching the battle. The little ship was taking a beating, and the media was asking loads of questions. Though I was very busy monitoring the dome, I answered the best I could.

"Freddy, how long can she keep taking a beating like that before her shields run out?"

"Not much longer. She doesn't have the power sources we have."

"Will the two Sycloyed ships be able to fight their way to Earth?"

"Not a chance. The fleet will take care of them long before that."

"Are you sure that our ships can harm them? They look really big and nasty."

I thought, *Well, that's a really professional way to put it.* What I said was, "Yes, I'm very sure."

"What happens if the little ship's shields run out before we can get there?"

"She'll be completely destroyed, but our ships should

be there very soon." Almost as soon as I said it, the two Sycloyed ships exploded into bits, and in a flash, two sleek shark-class ships showed up on the screen. One pulled up on the side of the little ship and placed a tractor beam onto her.

I said, "See? Our ships have firepower that far exceeds anything the Sycloyeds have."

The media were amazed at the ease and a little disappointed that it was over so quickly.

"Most battles," I added, "are over in just seconds. When you consider that the battle is in space, and any hole could cause major damage, if not total destruction, then space battles will normally be very short. Think of the battles between fighter squadrons. If they go head-to-head and don't try running, then the battle is very short. The squadron with the best pilots and the most protected ships comes out the winner very fast. What you just saw on the screens was the equivalent of two of our finest fighters going up against two World War I dirigibles." I let that sink in.

"Being in space is very dangerous. Being in a battle in space, especially without shields, is just short of suicidal. That's one of the reasons I invented shields before I sent up the first ship. I like living. The Sycloyeds have Great Ships, and they can take a lot of damage from navigational debris and such, but they have no shields. The two ships that destroyed them used only lasers—not even their most powerful weapons. I would bet that the captains of those two shark-class ships are just as surprised as you are."

I stopped what I was doing and turned to the media. "Some of our clairvoyance specials have dreamed about this fight and what is to come. We're at a junction."

The president interjected, saying, "We've been studying what the specials have said. The Sycloyeds have fought the peaceful races up until now. We are the first aggressive race they've encountered. If we give them the chance, they will develop ways to destroy us. Right now, they don't have a chance, but we are a silly race. In most of the clairvoyants' dreams, we allow the Sycloyeds to live, thinking we can change them and coexist. How arrogant. When that decision is made, in every dream we end up completely wiped out. All civilization, as we know it, is removed, and the Sycloyeds end up taking over all that we know. They will simply develop shields and weapons that will destroy us and then sanitize Earth. As we are not spread out yet, we present an easy and tempting target."

This brought silence from the media for a few minutes.

A short while later, the communications officer announced to the captain, "Incoming call from Earth Ship *Blue Fin*, Captain."

"Put her on screen, Comms."

On the screen, the captain of the *Blue Fin* appeared.

"Hi, Fred. Nice flying," said our captain. "I see you've got the Menseains."

"Nice to see you, too, Nickeli, and thanks. I see Freddy got that tug out of the locker. Tell him thanks. I just made five big ones. I knew he'd do it."

I smiled and said, "You're welcome, and tell the fool who bet against me to let me know next time so I can place a bet."

Fred laughed. "Good, you're there, Dr. Anderson. I'll do that. We have a guest who needs to talk with you. He says it's extremely important."

I asked, "If you don't mind, Captain?"

"Put him on, Fred."

The screen changed to a view of the Menseain ship's quarterdeck. It was a water tank with thousands of lights in colors and patterns that defied description. There were no sharp corners and no straight angles; everything was curved. We knew what it look liked aboard their ships from the documentation but nothing compared to seeing it live.

The increased noise of exclamation from the media was proof of the beauty we beheld. There were three Menseains in the cabin. The one on the left was working against the wall and was nearly upside down. The one on the right was very close and ducked when the one in the center motioned with a wing. The Menseain's wings radiated different colors, like a translucent butterfly, as it moved through the water. The torso was manlike but with fins and long, flat, webbed feet and hands. The center Menseain looked very strong, but at the same time he looked delicate, elflike. The one in the center looked up at a screen and started talking. The ship's translators worked fine, and I could hear him in English.

"Freddy, Envoy I am. Sent you from Bubble Maker were I. Friend yours sent me. Say you give shields him. Say you powerful very. Say you nice. See he right. Life mine, I thank for. Gone shields soon, if continue I. Understand you, I?"

"I understand. Why are you bringing the war to our little world?"

"Desirable not. Sad to this comes must. War lose soon. Sycloyeds' hate strong us against. planet home ours at they." His head dipped in a way that could only be extreme sadness. "Die children many. Help need or lose all. Contact worlds all. Know them we let. Help hope we us."

"Just a second, please." I turned to the president and said, "I need to go back to the base as quickly as possible."

"Why, Freddy?"

"I'm going to help my friend Bubble Maker. I will not let the Sycloyeds destroy the people who have been saving our lives for thousands of years. I owe them that help."

"*We* owe them that help, Freddy. Please tell him that we need to talk and will contact him shortly."

I asked, "What is your name, friend?"

"Silent Swimmer, I."

"Silent Swimmer, my people need to talk. You will get

help. We need to determine how much help you'll get. Please wait just a little."

"You, thank I. Wait I." He motioned with a wing, and the screen went back to the *Blue Fin*.

"Did you catch that, Fred?" our captain asked.

"Yes, I caught it, and so did the rest of the world and the fleet. The media is still broadcasting."

The president said, "Captain Nervloe, I need to talk to Congress right away."

"Communications."

"They're already calling her, Captain."

Captain Nervloe said, "Put them on screen."

Congressman Nathans stood tall on the screen and looked over the ship and then focused on the president. "Madam President."

"Congressman Nathans, it's nice to see you."

Congressman Nathans smiled and said, "We were watching, Madam President, and have already voted in the House and Senate. We have been talking about this possibility for nearly a year and have felt that if the war comes to us or if the Menseains ask for our help, then you won't have time for a vote. We voted in advance. You have all power to give them that help, Madam President. We are declaring war, and we are saying that we have an applied obligation to the Menseain race of mutual protection. Please, at all speed, help our friends."

"Thank you." The president turned to the captain. "Get me Admiral Penn."

"Coming up." Only seconds later, the screen changed to the quarterdeck of the ES *Hero*.

Admiral Penn stood on the quarterdeck. The *Hero* was the first cruiser-class ship we built. "Nice to see you, Madam President."

"Admiral Penn, were you watching?"

"Yes."

"I made you the admiral of the fleet for this exact reason. Leaving enough protection to cover Earth against attack, how many ships can you supply for this task?"

"Depends. Freddy, when can you let me have that carrier?"

"It's all yours, Admiral, and I can protect this solar system from all possible attacks."

Everyone turned to look at me. Admiral Penn asked, "Are you sure, Freddy?"

"Admiral, I can defeat the entire fleet if I need to, including the carrier. You wouldn't have a chance." I could sense that the admiral needed a little time to think, so I changed the subject to something less important. "Another subject, Admiral—we haven't named it yet. It's the first ship used to protect this system and all other worlds from oppression and annihilation. What do you think it should be called?"

He smiled and said, "The *Enterprise*."

"Can't do it, Admiral. I'm saving that name for my first research-class Great Ship."

I could see the thought and wonder of what that ship could be flash across his face. But disappointment was there also, and he said, "Then, as the politicians have voted in advance on this subject, let's name her after that great move. The ES *Thinking Ahead*."

Susan said, "Be serious, Admiral."

I paused and placed a finger to my temple in deep thought. Everyone was quiet. I looked up and said, "Actually, Susan, that's a great idea. What they have done is highly important and shows that they are thinking more about this world and its safety than the tiny problems of a single state. That was a very important move. Let's name if after their efforts. Why not the ES *Insight?* Earth Ship *Insight* or ESI. It's also the first ship to have specials stationed on her, correct?"

The admiral smiled. "That's very true. ES *Insight* it is. Including the ESI, we can float a full fleet of over three hundred ships, counting the fighters, and that's leaving ten good ships home as guard. No offense, Freddy, but I don't want to leave you with the burden. I know you can do it, but you have more important work. I want that AD available and out to us as quickly as possible."

"Consider it done." Under my breath, I asked Susan, "How'd he know about the AD?"

She whispered back, "The media was sending during lunch."

"Oh."

Admiral Penn said, "Fred, let me talk to Silent Swimmer."

The Menseains came back on the screen.

"Silent Swimmer, I am Admiral Penn. I am a personnel friend of Dr. Anderson and the commander of the Earth space fleet. Freddy has asked us to assist you in this battle. As we are speaking, the fleet is preparing to leave to join the battle against these Sycloyeds. I am sending every ship I have except ten. That's 150 warships, if you count small fighters. They will leave immediately. Another hundred or so ships will quickly follow, accompanied by our largest warship—it takes a little longer to get it ready. As you can see, two of our smaller ships were an easy match for the two that were chasing you. Please look at your monitors now."

The ES *Hero* was coming up quickly. Silent Swimmer and the other two Menseains swam back in shock. The *Hero* and the *Protectress* and her two sister ships were now only a few miles away from them, and they filled the Menseains' scanners.

"Ships, these. Help come now?"

"Yes, along with many others. We will pull you along with us. We are faster. You would slow us down."

I could feel their worry, and I added, "You wonder why we have not attacked you yet?"

"Normal, it is. Species yours. Weaker attack those."

"We've grown out of that. We don't attack our friends anymore."

He placed both his wings to cover his head in front, bowed, and said, "Oh, Great Swimmer praises Bubble."

Admiral Penn said, "It's time to leave. Fleet, lay in coordinates for Menseain. Warp seven. Engage now. I have approximately seventy-six hours to plan this out. I expect that carrier and the rest of the fleet to be right behind us, Freddy."

"We'll do our best, Admiral."

The captain of the *Folly* said, "Blast one for the home team, Admiral."

Admiral Penn said, "I hate war, and I hate battles. It's one of the things that makes me so good at it. If at all possible, I'll have this conflict over with before the carrier gets there."

The president ordered, "Don't stop at the Menseain home planet, Admiral. I don't want them deciding to spread out in another direction. If the ships are working out as well as we expect, then your orders are to take this all the way. I'm not a president who believes in leaving an enemy behind me to attack when I'm not looking, especially when I've been warned. You're in charge. Protect our friends, and finish this war permanently. I don't want to ever hear of a Sycloyed, except as history. Those are the only orders I'm giving you. Are we clear on that?"

"Understood, Madam President. Out."

The screen went blank.

The captain said, "Freddy, you and the team can take

one of the ship's shuttles back to base and get that carrier moving. I'll take care of the dome."

"Thanks, Captain." We headed back to help Admiral Ken Lasen prepare for takeoff.

✦

All the aliens looked shocked. Gray said, "The *Protectress* is the biggest Earth ship we've fought so far. Now we find that there are bigger and faster—the *Hero* and this *Insight!*"

Blue said, "Perhaps they were destroyed in the battle with the Sycloyeds. We have avoided that area of space. Eventually, we will have to battle these creatures."

Green said, "We will see, but I think these creatures will not give up so easily against these Sycloyeds."

Blue said, "The Sycloyeds should not be in this sector yet. I have told the Body Proper, and they will warn the fleet and ask for immediate reinforcements. Green, please continue."

Green said, "The Body Proper wishes me to show you what we know of this Admiral Penn and the admiral who is in charge of this ES *Insight*. It is bits and pieces from others, but the Body Proper warns that we will meet them soon."

CHAPTER 8

✦ ✦ ✦

UNDER WAY

On the ES *Insight*, Admiral Lasen was having a meeting with the other officers in his stateroom. Lt. Janet Dunner said, "She's a beautiful ship, Admiral Lasen."

The admiral thought about being the first admiral of the first space carrier and paid little attention to the small talk going on around the room. Women and children were what he was thinking about. *Being an admiral of a carrier that floats on water and having women sailors is one thing, but this is a completely new frontier. I thought I'd have months, maybe years, before my completely new crew would be heat-tested, but here we are, preparing to go to war against an experienced space-faring race that, by all accounts, has no mercy. Half my crew is women, and I have five children. The women aren't the problem. Give me a crew of all women, and I'd have the best crew in the fleet. It's when you put men and women together that the problems start."*

"I'm really worried about whether she'll fly," the lieutenant said.

That brought the admiral out of his private thoughts. "Lieutenant, I'll have no negative thoughts, please. Dr. Freddy Anderson himself has inspected every inch of this ship. She'll fly, all right. She'll be the fastest, most powerful ship in the known universe. I trust what Dr. Anderson has approved. What I don't trust is that we'll know how to run his equipment. The reports I get from the specials assigned to the ship are that most of the crew is unsure of what they're doing. We cannot afford mistakes, ladies and gentlemen. As soon as were up, I'll have hourly drills. Is that understood?

"Yes, sir."

"Good. Plan for it. Each shift is to hold drills eight hours a day. Do not overload them with other activities. I want them rested, with energy to burn when we get there. You have your orders."

Everyone left him in his stateroom. The suite was big enough that it included a separate bedroom, bath, walk-in closet, kitchen, conference room, and office. The room was highly comfortable, with carpet so thick and soft you'd lose your toes if you weren't careful. The pictures were expensive and covered up the controls needed during battle planning. The admiral's desk was big enough for two and was made from polished dark-wood-textured metal. His chair was the same dark metal and was on guides that kept it on the floor, even if gravity gave out, but also let him slide in and out.

He drifted off, thinking about everything that had happened to put him in this highly precarious situation.

One year ago, almost to the day, the president had called him in from a deployment. The admiral had flown off the aircraft carrier *America* and landed in Washington, thinking he was in some sort of trouble again. His career was somewhat rocky, as he refused to do anything the conventional way. He had just finished maneuvers with several other countries, and he'd tromped them. He was never where he was expected to be, and this ticked off everyone, including half his own fleet. In fact, the admiral had handled the exercise with only one-third of his ships. The rest he used for throwing the other admirals and countries off track. He ended up theoretically wiping out nearly all the other fleets' ships, while only losing one ship himself and pissing off the dozen other admirals that lost.

When he arrived in Washington, he reported directly to the White House. The president received him right away. Admiral Martin Penn was there. Admiral Penn was an old friend and Admiral Lasen's mentor. The two men fought and thought a lot alike. Admiral Penn was the only naval officer that Lasen ever looked up to. They greeted each other, and then the president dropped the hammer.

"A message has been sent to the carrier, telling your captain to take charge. You won't be back." Admiral Lasen was just about to apologize when she dropped the next hammer. She was looking out the window when she asked, "Admiral, you know about Dr. Freddy Anderson?"

"Yes, Madam President. Of course I know." *Who doesn't?* he thought.

"Then you are aware that Dr. Anderson is building a fleet carrier?"

He stood a little straighter. "No, ma'am, that I didn't know."

"He is, and I need an admiral to run it. It requires a lot of intensive training in engineering, working with specials and three-dimensional tactics. If you agree to try for this position, then you will need to be screened, mentally and physically, and approved first. If you pass, then you will spend the next year preparing with four other officers." She turned and looked at him right in the eyes. "Admiral, the world needs someone to take charge of this ship and protect this planet." She paused, staring at him with an intensity that could rival a desert sun. "We have company out there, Admiral—eight different races that we know of so far. We're hoping and praying that they're friendly, but if not, then at least two of them have the potential to remove our race from existence. Freddy has agreed to make this carrier on the understanding that its primary use is to help populate other worlds."

"I hope that's all we ever have to use it for, Madam President."

"And that's exactly why I want you to go through this training. I don't need a power-hungry, war-loving moron in control of the most powerful ship ever built. You pass those tests and become first in your class. That's an order, Admiral. Dismissed—both of you."

Once out in the hall, Admiral Lasen asked, "Martin, what's going on? I've never seen her like this. She's worried about something."

"Ken, I'm sorry for the abrupt way she's acting, but she has a lot on her mind. Freddy has invented and launched his first building-moving ship. Ken, it works! He dropped the first building on the moon just last week. The robots in his factory are building another destroyer-class ship. He is starting on a cruiser and a carrier. He's a special, and there's an uproar about specials throughout the world. There simply are not enough of them to go around. In this country, most are too young to work. People are afraid that the other countries are using them to undermine the rest of us. Most of the specials we find go to Freddy's home—and for good reason. He has helped almost all of them get over issues that we can't even comprehend. Still, the rest of the country is up in arms and accusing the president of taking all of them for herself."

"That's ridiculous."

"You know how the people are. They want it, and they want it now. You'd think they'd learn patience before they reached the age to vote. The president has to protect the specials, keep us out of war with other countries, and now prepare for a war with the Sycloyeds."

"She really thinks that's a possibility?"

"Not only a possibility, but the Congress is doing research, and so far it suggests that it's very likely. Earth happens to be right in their path. She's praying that we'll have time to prepare, but she can't be sure, and she's worried."

"We have some protection now, what with the *Protectress* and the other ships."

"True, and Freddy is working to help her. No one knows this, Ken, so don't let this out. There have been eight attempts on Freddy's life. The specials tell us that there are a lot of people who don't think we should go into space or don't like Freddy building weapons, and other countries don't like the idea that were pulling so far ahead of them in everything. Freddy has been great, and his hard work has saved our lives, but there are repercussions. He knows this and expects it. It's typical of him. He thinks it's 'silliness,' and he doesn't take it very seriously." Admiral Penn smiled and continued. "Unless, of course, the army tries something. I think he's looking for a reason to bloody their noses." They both laughed.

"Four countries have asked to become states, including Canada and Mexico," Admiral Penn said. "They want to be a bigger part of everything that's happening. England and Australia have presented Congress with a proposal that we change our name from the Unites States to Earth Federation. They are willing to join the Federation and are fully willing to become part of our new country. If that happens, then they get to vote, and in next election we could have an English or Australian president. Can you believe that? Freddy is inadvertently pulling this world together."

"Are they seriously thinking about doing any of this?"

"Yes, very seriously. Before we start colonizing other planets, the president would like it to be a lot more stable here at home. It would be good if the entire world was one country, but the likelihood of getting China and Russia to join is slim."

"This training—when will we start?" Admiral Lasen asked.

"We're starting now."

Admiral Lasen was ushered into a room with several people, including—as he soon found out—a psychologist, as well as children. At first, the kids were playing, but the moment the psychologist started talking, they became very serious and watched Admiral Lasen very closely.

The psychologist asked, "Admiral. It is admiral, isn't it?"

"Yes, but you can call me Ken."

The psychologist looked up with one eye. Three of the children giggled but a girl of about twelve gave them a look, and they instantly stopped. No words were exchanged, so it was clear that they were specials. I put my hand out to the girl and said, "Hello. I'm Admiral Ken Lasen. You're a special, aren't you?"

The girl extended her hand and said, "Welcome, Admiral Lasen. Yes, we all are. My name is Connie."

"It's nice to meet you, Connie." As they shook hands, a little boy reached up and put both hands around Ken's arm and lifted his feet. "Well, who do we have here?"

Connie covered her mouth with one hand and looked at the boy. He looked at her and then looked at me, pouting. I raised my arm, lifting him up, asking, "What's your name, young man?"

"I'm Johnny. You're nice."

"Well, thank you." Two of the other children took hold of my legs, and the rest pulled me down. We played, laughing and tickling for only a few minutes before the doctor ruined the fun.

Loudly clearing of his throat, he said, "I don't have all day, Admiral."

Ken could sense that the doctor did not enjoy the children, and that disappointed him greatly. The man seemed bored, rude, and a little intimidating toward the children. Ken took offense with this attitude. He stood, picked up his hat, and walked briskly toward the doctor. Connie was there instantly. She put out a hand to stop me, and then turned to the doctor.

"The admiral is very upset with the way you just treated us. He looks at us as if we were his own grandchildren. He misses his wife, who has been dead for several years now." She placed a hand on Ken's arm, asking forgiveness for bringing up such a sad issue. "He does not care if we are specials or not. To him, that means that we are children with an extra burden." She turned to Ken and said, "You are correct on that, Admiral." She turned back to the doctor and said, "He has a tiny bit of empathy and can detect that you are a little hostile toward us. You may continue with the interview." She turned toward Ken and said, "No, Admiral, you will not have him replaced. We use his attitude for our own purposes." She walked back to the rest of the children.

The psychologist looked up at Ken from his desk and said, "Have a seat, Admiral."

It was them that Ken understood that the psychologist was not the one in charge. Connie was, and Ken had just been tested.

The psychologist asked, "Ready, Admiral?"

"I suppose so."

"Good. I have twelve questions for you. Please answer every question verbally and in fifty words or more. The children need to ascertain what's in your mind with each question. Don't lie, don't tell half-truths, and don't try to mislead. They will know instantly and will report that you were uncooperative." He asked a dozen questions, some expected and some very surprising.

"Explain your attitude toward the United States."

That's easy, Ken thought. "I have loved the US all my life. I have been to nearly all other countries and have found no better place."

"Explain your attitude toward the world."

This was harder for him, but he said, "All countries are filled with good people. In some countries, people are pushed into making bad decisions. In others, the top few become greedy, and that makes it hard on the others. Every country has something to endear it to me, but all countries, including the US, can improve."

"If you had the chance and the power, what things would you change about the world and the way people act?"

"No one man has the right to change the way people are or act. As a people, the people must change if they so desire. No man has the right to change them, even if he has the power. To do so would be immoral, and he wouldn't be doing it for the people. He would be doing it for himself."

"How many people have you killed, for what reasons, and did you enjoy it?"

"Outside of wars or skirmishes that placed me under orders, none. I have killed during several legal actions by following my orders. I never enjoy harming another, but I don't lose sleep over it either."

"How do you feel about Dr. Anderson and his inventions?"

"I follow Dr. Anderson, like everyone else. He is a remarkable young man. I owe him my life."

"Tell me about a time when you wanted to get even with someone. Tell me how, when, why, and how you planned to get even, regardless of whether you carried it through."

Answering that questions took Ken some time, as he'd gotten even with quite a few people in his life.

"Explain how you envision children—how you think

of them, what you enjoy thinking about when you think of them?"

Here, Connie interjected, "There is no need for him to answer those questions. We have already removed the answers."

The psychologist nodded and then asked, "In what situation would you destroy an entire race of people?"

Ken had to think about that one but then answered, "If that race were a menace to the human race, or if I was under logical orders from someone I knew was not a nut case, then I would destroy the race."

"Have you ever cheated?"

He took several minutes to answer this one and told several stories that had the children laughing nearly constantly.

"Do you ever lie in your reports, and if so, why?"

Ken's answer to this was a resounding yes, and then he explained, "You don't ruin someone's career and life over something small, especially if you believe that person has learned his lesson."

The doctor said, "Last question, Admiral. Do you want power?"

The first thing that came to mind was, *Trick question.* His answer was simple and truthful. "Do I need the power to protect my family? Yes. Do I need the power to protect the country and world I love? Yes. Do I want to have power? No. I would love to be fishing, golfing, playing with my grandchildren, or anything else. Do I need power? Yes. I need to ensure the freedom of my family, my country, and the world for this generation and all generations to come."

Connie stood up and said, "The interview is over, Admiral. You pass. However, I would caution you that you need to spend time around more specials to learn how to shield, as your mind is far too wide open. Please go through that door." She pointed toward the left. Ken shook her hand and ruffled Johnny's hair.

He spent the next three weeks undergoing a complete physical. After that, it was off to Pensacola, Florida, for training.

The naval base in Pensacola was legendary for its pilot training, but now, with spaceships, they were developing a different kind of pilot. Ken trained in dogfighting tactics, flight squadron tactics, submarine strategies, and three-dimensional chess that could go in any direction. The pieces could move in any orientation and be upside down and backward. Facing counted in this chess game, and if your piece was not facing in the correct direction, others could sneak up on you, or you could not attack. He constantly trained in any tactic that would help to change his mental thought pattern from two-dimensional to more than three-dimensional. In space, it's not just up, down, backward, forward, and side to side. It included ship angles, direction, and speed. He studied history, including all about the Sycloyeds and their way of fighting; Anderson Engineering; and math. For Ken, that was the fun part. It was completely new and matched his personality, as he excelled there. He always loved anything out of the ordinary. He took the championship in the chess game every month there. He found the rest to be boring, but he completed everything and graduated second in the class.

The only reason Ken was in charge was that the specials flunked the top person the day before graduation. They also dropped out two others. That left Ken with an executive officer and an operations officer—Sally Prox and Kim Lee, respectively. When Ken first arrived at training, he had no idea that three of the six in training were female. Now, he had two of them to help run the ship, and he was extremely glad. Both were highly capable.

My ship, he thought. When he walked out of his cabin to check on his ship, two marines followed, but he thought nothing of it. He went into the communication room and received a report on the condition of the ship and crew. He checked weapons and engineering and ran into Freddy on the main deck in an argument with an ensign that Ken recognized as a new medical assistant. Freddy and Ken had become close over the last two weeks, with Freddy training Ken on several issues and the possible capabilities of the ship.

Ken walked up to the two and asked, "Is this ensign causing you problems, Dr. Anderson?"

The ensign's eyes widened, and when he heard that the civilian he was yelling at was *the* Dr. Freddy Anderson, he nearly fainted.

Freddy reached up and touched the ensign on the head, while saying disappointedly, "I get that a lot."

The ensign straightened up and stood at attention.

"Report to my quarters at 1900 hours tonight, Ensign," Ken said. "What's this all about, Freddy?"

"I'm trying to take these new PAADs to medical so that I can store them away properly and give some training on them. I'm expected. That person"—he pointed to the ensign—"thinks that I don't have clearance to be aboard *my* ship! I was just about to teleport myself around him or teleport him off my ship. I hadn't made up my mind which to do."

"Well, Ensign?" Ken asked.

"I'm the medical person who was supposed to give escort to the inventor and builder of the AD and PAADs. I didn't realize this child could possibly be him."

"Where have you been for the last few years? Freddy's been plastered all over the news. Still is."

"In college and working through internship. I don't even own a television, Admiral, sir."

Freddy said, "He's telling the truth, but what he's not saying is that he thought I was just a kid who snuck on and would not even give me the chance to explain. When I said I was Freddy, he laughed at me."

Ken raised his eyes and said, "Interesting." He bent down and straightened Freddy's collar. It was all tucked in. "Freddy, it would help if your collar wasn't turned under. The ensign could not see what rank you hold. Ensign, I want you to bring your medical officer with you when you report to my office. Let me escort you personally, Freddy. I wanted to check out the medical facilities again anyway. You can follow if you want, Ensign. In fact, I'd suggest it."

Freddy wasn't smiling; he looked worried. Ken remembered what the captain of home base had said during introductions: *"Freddy does not like to see anyone harmed in any way."* Ken leaned down and said, "Don't worry. I won't do anything bad. I'll just give him enough to remember that he should be a little bit more courteous."

"Thanks, sir."

"You're welcome, Freddy."

Ken dropped Freddy off in medical and continued on his rounds. While he was in the passageways leading to one of the crew quarters, a chief came running up. "Call from the president, sir."

"I'll take it in my cabin, Chief."

"It's urgent, sir."

"Bring it up on the nearest screen, Chief."

Only a hundred feet away was one of the flat panels that Freddy imported from a company in Austin, Texas. The president was on screen by the time Ken reached it.

"Yes, Madam President?"

"Admiral, when can you depart?"

"As soon as you need."

"Leave now. Congress is trying to keep half the fleet back to protect Earth."

"That would be a mistake, ma'am."

"You and I both know it. Leave!" The screen went blank.

Ken then told his clear dot to put him in contact with the operations officer.

"On line, sir."

"Good. Prepare to get under way."

"Yes, sir. Are you headed to the bridge?"

"Not yet. Tell the executive officer that she has the bridge until I return. I'm headed to medical to personally escort Freddy off this ship. If we inadvertently end up taking him with us, we're all up for court-martial. Knowing Freddy, he'll try to come along. Get all personnel onboard. We're taking off in ten minutes."

"Yes, sir."

"Dot, contact Captain Susan James."

"This is Shop, Admiral. Captain James sends her best. She's on her way to the forward gangplank. She knows what you're doing, and she'll ensure Freddy is taken care of."

"Good." Ken was turning the corner to the medical facility when Freddy came out.

Looking at Ken, he said with a slight pout, "The ship's engines are on, Admiral. Everyone just became very busy. You're leaving, aren't you?"

"Yes, Freddy. You need to depart the ship before Captain James gets mad at me."

"Yes, I know," He sounded a little upset. "She's coming up the plank now. I think she'd shoot this ship down before she let me go anywhere. Very disappointing."

"I think you're right."

We were already headed toward the forward quarterdeck, traveling down the transport tube. We stepped off at the correct connection and were shot toward the port side at nearly eighty miles an hour. Only seconds later, we were at the forward port quarterdeck, and there was Captain James.

Freddy said, "Hi, Mother," and gave her a big hug. "I finished those PAADs and gave then to medical."

"That's great, sweetheart. I'm sure they'll be very helpful. We have to leave now. You need to help the admiral get the carrier out of the hangar."

"That's set on automatic, and you know it. You just want me off my ship." Freddy turned around and said to Ken, "You take care of my ship, Admiral. I want her back in one piece." Then he smiled and, raising a hand, said, "Shields up."

Ken raised his right hand and repeated, "Shields up." As he watched Freddy and the captain walking off, he couldn't help but think, *He doesn't even know that he's changed the way people say good-bye all over the world.*

✦

Gray was pacing back and forth with his head down. Worried, he said, "They have a genius admiral."

Blue said, "We attacked quickly and decisively. They were taken completely by surprise. We did not find these admirals, nor did we find this ship, the *Insight*, or the *Hero*. They are either dead by our hands or by the Sycloyeds. There is nothing to worry about."

Gray said, "As you wish, sire. But you do not mind if I do my job, do you?" He called another Gray to him. "Warn the fleet that we have evidence that the Earth force we attacked may not have been their main fleet. Tell them I said to make haste to our main fleet and double those reinforcements." The other Gray left.

Blue said, "That is expensive and not necessary."

Big Yellows said, "You keep the civilians happy, Blue. Let Gray protect the empire. Green, continue."

CHAPTER 9

✦ ✦ ✦

BATTLE

The ship was secured with a full complement onboard, and reports of readiness were coming in from each department by the time Admiral Ken Lasen reached the bridge.

"Admiral on the bridge!"

Everyone snapped to attention, except the critical areas.

The admiral said, "Continue, XO. Take her out."

The ESI was three miles long and nearly three-quarters of a mile wide. Even as big as she was, she took up only about half the building area in Freddy's home. The screens came up, and Ken could clearly see her rising off the floor of the shop. Teleporting out of the shop went smoothly. There wasn't even the sound of stressed metal. Everything felt solid.

The ESI took to space with no problems, only sixty-three hours after war was declared. She took three hours in space to ensure that she worked perfectly and then shipped out at warp eleven toward the Menseain home world.

True to his word, Admiral Penn left ten ships stationed around Earth. All were the bulky shuttle types, and it was hoped to be enough firepower and shielding power to protect Earth.

The fleet showed up outside the Menseain solar system. The carrier ESI showed up only minutes behind them. Admiral Penn transferred his flag to the ESI, and the battle started—although it wasn't really a battle. The fleet walked right through them like they were made of paper. The smallest fighters could take out the Sycloyeds' ships so easily and quickly that there was no chance for them to flee. The only problem was the base ships. They had thousands of little fighters, and though they could hardly harm Earth's ships by themselves, they could gang up on one of the smaller ones and cause damage. This was the tactic that the Sycloyed fleet used. When a squadron of fighters flew in, all firepower from the Sycloyeds would concentrate on the lead ship. Admiral Penn saw this immediately and ordered all squadrons to include one "drop ship." The drop-ship fighter was a three-man unit that Freddy designed for landing troops. He made the drop ships with extra shielding so that they could drop straight down through the atmosphere at full speed and right into the middle of battle with their cargo still intact. When the Sycloyeds attacked the drop ship, it just sat there, as the rest of the fighters picked off the Sycloyed fighters. With all the dogs fighting, it took a long time to wipe them out. The admiral stationed ships to shield the planet from falling debris. The entire war, a war that the Menseains had been fighting for over one hundred years, was over in just eighteen hours twenty-three minutes.

When the fighting at the Menseain home world was over, Admiral Penn called down to the planet and asked the Menseains if the one called Bubble Maker was there. It seemed that "Bubble Maker" was a very common name, and it took some explaining to get the correct Bubble Maker.

They found him in a hospital-type of water facility, trying to help the Menseains that were injured.

The screen came on, and Bubble Maker was swimming there with what appeared to be several top-ranking officials. There clearly was great fear among them. Looking sad, he said, "I am the one called Bubble Maker. My most sincere apologies, but I do not have the authority to surrender to you." Admiral Penn's face showed no emotion to this unexpected possibility.

"Bubble Maker, I am Admiral Penn, fleet admiral of the Earth fleet."

Bubble Maker perked up. "Earth? My Earth?"

Admiral Penn did smile at this. "If you mean the Earth that you and your kind have protected for thousands of years, then yes." Then he asked Bubble Maker, "Are you the one that sent for help from Dr. Anderson?"

His eyes widened. "Friend Anderson? Yes, I did. Silent Swimmer, my brother—is he still alive?"

"Silent Swimmer and his ship are out here, protected by my shielding. They are safe and can return home at any time. The Sycloyeds' fleet has been removed from your system. Freddy sends his greetings. He has sent us here to end this killing of his friends. It is my job to destroy the Sycloyeds so that there is no chance of another attack. Are they attacking any other planets?"

"Yes. We have five major systems that they are systemically destroying. Can you help us?"

"Yes. We have the coordinates of all your systems. We will be back when we've removed the Sycloyeds from them." He raised a hand and said, "Friends."

Bubble Maker raised his hand and wing and said, "Great friends."

The admiral gave orders, and the fleet dispersed into ten separate groups. Each group sent reports home. Most the world sat glued to their chairs as they watched the fleet tear through the rest of the enemy. The fleet left no Sycloyeds alive. They scoured over two hundred planets, and every one that the Sycloyeds were on became empty when the fleet started their approach. The queens were quick to abandon the planets and flee. That set them up as perfect targets. Only a couple of planets were left occupied. The admiral sent back the ESI for ground troops that the generals gladly supplied. Shuttles were stationed to those planets to help resupply the troops.

✦

Gray said, "It does not sound like they were losing that war. This is not good."

Yellows asked, "How many of their ships did we destroy?"

Gray said, "Twenty-three. Why?"

Green said, "Counting small fighters, they had over 250 ships. And the *Protectress* was one of the outdated types."

Gray said, "The shields on the *Protectress* were stronger than anything we have ever encountered. It took the combined power of four base ships to take her out. Yet I would bet this ES *Insight* has better shields. This is a great worry." Gray left.

Blue looked at Big Yellows and asked, "Did we destroy their fleet or not? Because of the weapons on their planet, we could not attack Earth. Mars was wide open, and we took a lot of creatures from there. They are very mad. If their fleet is still out there, we could be in dark trouble."

Big Yellows said, "We put most of those people back. We were after this one. We only know this much thanks to Green's probing. We took out twenty-three ships, but they have hundreds. We need more information."

Blue said, "Two of our fleets are across the galaxy, fighting in other wars. Our home is protected by the third fleet only. Most of the first fleet was destroyed in the conflict with Earth, and now we find out that we were not fighting their fleet!"

Big Yellows said, "Our intelligence about this world called Earth has been limited by their scanners. They were finding us, and our spies had to flee. After the attack on the mother ship, no information has come out of this sector. We were working on old information."

Blue said, "That old information may have just gotten us killed. Let's hope we can find a way out of this situation. Continue, Green."

Green added a tentacle and started the probing again.

I continued what I was doing. I had kept all controls reading the same and bypassed this tank. It was now a matter of time and rest and hoping their backup did not kick in.

Gray walked back in, and he looked happy.

CHAPTER 10

✦ ✦ ✦

HEROES

On the screens above my head, I watched as reports from other humans were being watched by the gray alien. Meanwhile, Green continued to probe me, and I gave him just enough to keep them interested.

"Base one, this is Lieutenant Tomius of the supply shuttle *Lion's Pride*. Come in, base one."

"*Lion's Pride*, this is base one. Sergeant Keal, here. Use standard vectors and come down on this frequency. It's good to hear from you. How's the fleet doing?"

"Reports are that we've lost only one ship so far, but there are many banged up, and the death toll is mounting."

"How'd we lose the ship, Lieutenant?"

"The ship was taken out by another species. Reports say we came to close to a planet that, unknown to us, was protecting itself from anything and everything. When one of our fighters closed in, a beam shot out from the planet and cut it in half. The foolish pilot did not have his shields up."

"Heck, Lieutenant, even we know better than that. We may have other hostiles out there, then?"

"Definitely, Sergeant, but I don't think these were hostiles."

"Why not?"

"Apparently, we stationed two small ships in that system to watch, but because of the planetary defenses, the fighters had to station themselves in less-than-optimum positions. Several days later, eight Sycloyed ships flew into the system. The two Earth ships destroyed them quickly and then resumed positions. The world below must have seen the conflict, as they sent an apology for destroying our fighter and invited our ships to position themselves better. They made promises that they would not attack again. The fighters reported that down on the planet, they could see hundreds of signs of celebration. An admiral was sent aboard the ES *Champion* to initiate talks."

"That's great. You realize how many intelligent life-forms we've encountered so far? Just think; two years ago I would have bet you everything that we were the only intelligent life-form in the universe. And now we've encountered seventeen different species."

"Make that twenty-three to date."

There was an appreciative whistle over the comms. "Twenty-three. How many planets have been found that we can colonize?"

"Right now? Hard to say. Some planets are up for debate as to whether the life-forms on them are intelligent, and six planets are far too deadly. There is scuttlebutt that one planet has far too many predators that think we humans make a good snack."

There was laughter over the link.

"One planet has an unstable system. Great planet, but each year it circles closer to its sun. Last I heard, there are 146 confirmed planets that none of the others species are claiming. Of those, eight are ideal for colonization, and two are close to Earth."

"Close to Earth?"

"Well, close enough using Dr. Anderson's ships. Why? You volunteering to be one of the first colonists? I thought they taught you better than that in boot camp."

The sergeant laughed, "Sure. I'd love to, what with the world getting more and more crowded and resources becoming scarce. You bet I would. I come from a long line of farmers. I'd love to start farming on a planet that helps wipe out world hunger."

"Great—sign up for the planet they're calling Oreo."

"Oreo?"

"Sure. The bugs confiscated it and replanted. Never had to drop a single bomb, as they evacuated immediately. The planet is almost exactly like Earth, and it's all farmland and forest. They say it's a paradise. Some wanted to call it Eden."

"Why did they call it Oreo?"

"Weirdest thing I've ever seen, and that's saying a lot. Even the planetologists are baffled. Oreo is sandwiched between two suns."

"Wow! How is that possible?"

"The scientists are still trying to determine how that could happen. Apparently, the two suns rotate around each other, and the planet rotates at the perpendicular between the two. Don't ask me the details. It's far beyond me. I thought the gravity would tear the planet apart. The planet has a seventeen-hour day, no night, and a 561-day year with no seasons. The temperature is an average eighty-one degrees Fahrenheit over 60 percent of the land mass. As everything is so stable—rain seems to be gentle and comes in waves so that watering is not necessary. The big thinkers are still trying to figure out something bad about the planet."

"What? Why?"

"Millions have applied for colonization, Sergeant, and they're trying to discourage some of them."

"I have competition, then."

"Big time. But I don't think anyone is going to be colonizing anything until the heads of Earth can figure out how to control it."

"Control it?"

"The colonization and the people that colonize. They are working on who is going to be in charge, who they report to, etc. Believe me; it would come to war if it wasn't for the United States being so far ahead of everyone else that they would not stand a chance—and they know it. The president of the United States has stated that she cannot trust others and that they have proven this many times in the last year. Only members of the Earth force will populate these planets and be in charge. The entire world is in an uproar. England, Canada, and Mexico have petitioned to join the Earth force. Still, many others are extremely upset."

"You'd think they'd put away their petty political crap and jump on the bandwagon."

"You'd think. I'm down in four, three, two, one."

"You have the PAADs with you?"

"I have an AD on the shuttle and five PAADs with medical personnel to handle them."

"Thank the gods. Everyone here is sick as a dog. Eight have died, and others are not expected to live through the night. An escort is there to meet you. Be careful of the dragons."

"Dragons?"

"Yeah. We have dragons. They are the intelligent life on this planet. Any idea why the Sycloyeds didn't sanitize this planet?"

"No, none at all."

✦

Gray said, "ES *Champion*. Another ship we did not know about."

Blue said, "They did not lose their war."

Green asked, "Did we not decide to leave the Sycloyeds alone? What was the reasoning behind that decision?"

Gray looked embarrassed. "We are already fighting two other wars."

Blue asked, "What were our thoughts on a war with the Sycloyeds?"

Gray said, "We would destroy them without problem, but it would spread us thin. With the undead and machines on our flank, it would not be a good choice."

Green said, "The choice is being removed. Listen to this."

CHAPTER 11

✦ ✦ ✦

CHANGE OF PLAN

"Admiral Lasen, we are receiving a report from one of our scouts, the *Maco Five*. They've found something. Something big."

"Put it on the overhead, Comms."

An excited but scared voice came on the overhead. "I can't believe the size of this thing. Is anyone hearing this? My scanners say it's—just a second. Verified. The thing is over twenty-four kilometers in diameter. Crap, I wish Anderson would have programmed these things for miles! I have no idea how big that is."

A teasing female voice came on. "You Irish idiot. Dr. Anderson did. Just a second, and I'll adjust it for you. How's that?"

"Fifteen miles! *Wow!* That thing is fifteen miles in diameter."

Admiral Lasen asked, "Comms, who is running that ship?"

"Lieutenant Junior Grade Ryan O'Connor, sir."

"Comms, put it on the two-way."

"Aye aye, sir. You have two-way, sir."

"Lieutenant O'Connor, this is Admiral Lasen."

"What the—? Look here, fool. I don't know who you are, but I'm going to report—"

"O'Connor!" the female voice yelled. "That signal carries the friend-or-foe signal of the ES *Insight*!"

"Um … crap. There goes my promotion. Hello, Admiral Lasen. It's nice to hear from you, sir."

"Report! You have something out there that's fifteen miles in diameter, Lieutenant? What is it?"

"It's a ship, sir. Actually, we have several ships. I would guess to say an entire fleet."

"Sycloyeds?"

"What?"

The female whispered, "Bug ships, you fool. Bug ships. And stop shaking. I can't believe you. You attack ships ten times our size without a thought and shake at the sound of the admiral's voice."

The admiral gave the voice-cut-off signal, and communications acknowledged. "Communications, who is the female on that ship?"

Communications anticipated the request and had it on her screen. "It's a three-man crew, Admiral. The female is Master Chief Gunner's Mate Julia Jones. She was placed onboard to keep Lieutenant O'Connor and Fire Technician Petty Officer First Class Bob Norman in line."

Admiral Lasen said, "Two-way communication, please." As soon as communications gave the signal, the admiral took over. "Master Chief, report!"

"Aye aye, sir. There are fourteen of the large colonization ships, eight of the carriers, and they appear to have full complement. There are twenty-six of the smaller battleships and eighty-one destroyer escorts. The large ship is protected by the rest. She appears to be heading toward a planet fourth out from this sun. Several of the fighters are already attacking the surface. It seems like they already know exactly where to strike."

"What's that?" asked the petty officer.

Admiral Lasen turned to the captain and said, "Get me a dead reckoning on that ship, and turn the fleet to that course at all speed. Notify Admiral Penn. Continue, Master Chief."

"Admiral, the planet is defending. Over a thousand missiles just left the planet's surface, and they are slowly heading out toward the Sycloyeds. Admiral, those missiles will never hit. It's late-twentieth-century technology, at best. The planet is doomed, if that's the best they have."

"Master Chief, we have your position, and the fleet is under way. You lie low, and report until further orders." Admiral Lasen turned his attention to the quarterdeck. "Captain, what's our estimated time of arrival?"

"Three two minutes—that's thirty-two minutes, Admiral."

"Captain, that planet may not have thirty-two minutes. They know our tactics and speeds now. They have just enough time to destroy the planet and leave before we get there. There must be something important about the planet."

"Any faster, sir, and we leave the rest of the fleet behind. As it is, we're dragging many of the slower ships with us."

The operations officer interjected, "I've been thinking about that, sir. We could bring in several of the larger ships and carry them with us, using the tractor beams. We'd be taking a chance, but they would never believe that we can bring most of the fleet to bear that fast. We may not be able to save that planet, but they won't have time to disperse and disappear."

The captain said thoughtfully, "That may work, and we could be there in eight minutes."

Admiral Lasen ordered, "Do it. But go past, and come in from the other side of the sun. And sound general quarters."

Six minutes later, Maco Five reported, "Admiral, this is *Maco Five*. The big ship has stationed itself in high orbit, and the smaller ships have scattered. Something's happening. My God!" There was a long pause.

"*Maco Five*? Master Chief, report!"

"One shot, Admiral. That's all it took. One shot, and the entire surface of the planet is on fire, water and all. There is steam billowing up from the oceans, but the fire is not going out. It looks like the mother ship is powering up again. She is turning toward the outward planets like she is waiting for something. The other ships are hiding behind—"

Only the sad, lonely sound of static came from the intercom.

Communications said, "*Maco Five, Maco Five* ... come in, *Maco Five*." Nothing. No answer.

Admiral Penn entered the quarterdeck.

"Admiral on deck!"

"Carry on." Admiral Penn placed a hand on Lasen's shoulder. "I've been listening. That was a brave crew and a great loss. Either they were running without shields to minimize the chance of discovery, or the enemy has a new weapon."

The captain said, "Standard operation procedure, Admiral. Shields up at all times."

"Then let's consider it a new weapon. Warn the fleet. Tactics are to change to 2B immediately."

"Aye aye, Admiral. We are out of light speed in thirty seconds. You're on communications and open to the entire fleet. Orders, sir?"

"Stay back from that mother ship. Hide behind planets, and spread out the moment we arrive so she doesn't have an easy group of targets. Take out her protection first, and then we will destroy her from a distance and behind cover."

They dropped out on the sun side of the mother ship. It was apparent they surprised the Sycloyed mother ship, as she and all her escorts were easy targets, hiding on the wrong side of the planets as they were. It was almost like they were framed for the fleet. Half her escorts were destroyed before she could turn around to fire her planet-destroying weapon; however, she had no targets as the fleet hid behind other planets. She fired anyway, and another planet was set on fire. Two of Earth's smaller ships were on the other side and too close. The shields could not hold up to the sun's intensity of the fire with which they were now surrounded. Their shields collapsed, and the two ships were destroyed.

Admiral Penn quickly warned, "Stay back from the planets." The warning was not necessary, as the scanners showed that the ships were destroyed, and the entire fleet knew. One of the special children collapsed when over six hundred brave sailors instantly died. After that, the mother ship was never given another target.

The fighters had a difficult time, as the weapons on the larger Sycloyed ships could weaken and eventually destroy their smaller shields. Six or seven of Earth's fighters, however, could quickly take out the destroyers and did so until only the carriers and the mother ship were left.

The carriers encircled the mother ship, protecting her. Their fighters swarmed around the mother ship, keeping all missiles from hitting. The *Insight* fired missile after missile, and each one was met by a fighter. The problem was that they had more fighters than the *Insight* had missiles. In addition, the carriers would find a target and fire their new weapon, which did not destroy but somehow removed the shields.

The next shot, if you were foolish enough to stick around, would penetrate the hull. There also was the mother ship to contend with. She systematically shot every planet, so the *Insight* would have less room to hide.

Admiral Penn said, "Looks like the clairvoyants were correct. They've developed a way to destroy us."

Admiral Lasen smiled and said, "Dr. Anderson's new toy?"

"I think it's time. Don't you?"

"Yes, sir." Admiral Lasen turned to the captain and said, "Power up the antigravity guns, and prepare the fleet to fire all missiles."

The orders went out, and everyone waited in anticipation. Admiral Lasen said, "Good. The mother ship is pointing away from us. Captain, bring us out, and point us toward the mother ship."

"Aye aye, Admiral."

The ES *Insight* moved smoothly out toward the mother ship. Admiral Lasen ordered, "Fire all missiles." The screens displayed a hundred missiles heading toward the mother ship. Admiral Lasen saw the gunner's hand move toward the firing button. "Wait for it! Wait for it. Wait … for … it …"

Enemy fighters were now moving away from the mother ship toward the missiles, one suicide fighter for each missile.

Admiral Penn said, "You have to respect their loyalty."

Admiral Lasen said, "Wait for it … *now!*"

The gunner hit the button, and a wide beam shot out from the *Insight*, striking all enemy ships. Instantly the fighters broke off like their navigation equipment had stopped working. The carriers and the mother ship started drifting, and the enemy escorts were drifting, which opened great holes in the mother ship's protection. The missiles were locked on to the mother ship so they swerved around the now-drifting ships and struck the mother ship full on. She blew apart in a tremendous fireball that took out the rest of the enemy fleet and would have taken out several of Earth's ships, if not for the pilots' quick reflexes.

Admiral Penn said, "Captain, send out messages to the rest of the fleet. Let them know what happened here and the tactics to fight this new situation. Let them know that this may have been the only group with the new technology, but don't count on it. Be prepared and ready for ambushes. Then meet me and Admiral Lasen in the ready room. We need to discuss new tactics."

✦

Gray said, "They did not use that weapon against us."

Blue said, "We have not met their carrier yet."

Gray said, "We are more powerful. I am not worried. We will met this new threat and destroy it easily."

Yellows and Blue looked at Gray, wondering if he was telling the truth. Gray motioned for another Gray to attend him. He whispered, "I want those reinforcements, *now!*"

Little Yellows asked me, "Are we in trouble, little one?"

I smiled and said, "We never give up."

C H A P T E R   1 2

✦ ✦ ✦

AMBUSHED

Ensign Johnny Wearon scrambled into the pilothouse of the tiny scout ship, the *Thresher Eight*. "I rigged the communications system to at least receive, sir. We still cannot transmit. We have a message from Admiral Penn, sir."

"I'm busy!"

Another hit rocked the ship as it fled at breakneck speed through the asteroid cluster.

"Captain, shields are down to 33 percent."

"Great! Take energy from anything—life support, weapons, communications, and medical; anything except forward scanners and engines. It won't get us much, but it may buy us some time."

"Aye aye, Captain."

"What's the message, Johnny?"

"The admiral has encountered the enemy and they … sir, there's a lot of tactical information here, but it comes down to this: the enemy has new weapons, and we are to watch out for ambushes."

"Oh, wonderful! Day late and dollar short, Admiral. We have over twenty fighters and two destroyers on our tail. Anything in there that could help in our current"—the shipped rocked with another blast—"situation?"

Tentatively, he said, "We could turn and fight, sir."

"With what, Ensign? We are out of missiles, and our energy weapons have been diverted to the shields."

The petty officer in the science seat said enthusiastically, "Yes, but our shields are now up to 100 percent, sir." In a less enthusiastic tone, he added, "Temporarily."

The captain said, "We need to do something quick. We're running out of asteroids to hide in."

The petty officer said, "Ram them."

"What?"

"Ram them, sir. With our shields at full, we could take out at least one."

The captain thought quickly. "Great idea! But not like you think. We ram the weapons on the destroyer so it cannot penetrate our shields. If we live through that, we run like hell and warn the fleet."

"Sir!"

"Strap in! I want all energy except engines to the shields, including gravity."

"Yes, sir!" Both the ensign and the petty officer strapped in. "Ready, sir."

"Great. Here we go."

The captain slingshot the ship around a large asteroid, picking up as much speed as possible from the asteroids' little gravity. The ship was now on a collision course with the larger of the two destroyers. The fighters tried to get in the way, but the captain maneuvered the ship, expertly dodging and ducking constantly, until the only thing between the destroyer and his ship was the debris from the asteroids they destroyed to get to him.

To the crew's surprise, the destroyers fired frantically,

not allowing their weapon to fully charge; therefore, they had no effect on the shields.

"Captain! We're moving in too fast!"

"No, we are not! We just need to—"

Both the others threw their arms up and covered their heads as the *Thresher* slid sideways, ramming into the weapon on the front of the destroyer, and then shot off in another direction.

A wave of intense energy hit them from the back, so the captain flipped the ship around and was stunned to see that the destroyer they had just hit was missing its entire front section.

The ensign exclaimed, "You see that!"

The captain said, "Yes. It seems their weapon has a weakness."

"Captain, the other destroyer is pulling off and taking the fighters with him. Shall we pursue?"

"No. We need to get this information back to the fleet. Set course for the rendezvous point at Damien. Full speed."

The ensign said, "We may not make it, Captain."

"Plotted and set," the petty officer informed.

"We'll make it, Ensign. We have to. Engage."

✦

Blue said, "They are brave."

Gray said, "To the point of suicide, when needed. They are hardened warriors."

Blue said, "I say again that they would make great allies. They would do well in the undead wars."

Gray looked pleased with himself and very confident. He said, "We shall see. I think they will be surprised at the power we can bring to them. I think they will bow down to us and fight for us."

Blue said, "I do not think they will fight for anyone except themselves."

I said to Little Yellows, "I am confused my friend. Are the Grays your wayward children? It seems they have a lot of growing up to do. Our children who start out as bullies tend to act the same way until someone smacks them down hard. Then they grow up."

Little Yellows said, "Quickly, pen mate. Take over."

Big Yellows took hold of me, and Little Yellows sat on the floor, laughing so hard they were both in tears. Big Yellows was smiling and asked, "What?"

Little Yellows took a moment to calm down and said, "The creature wanted to know when the Gray would grow up. He thinks the Gray is immature."

All started laughing except Gray. With an evil grin on his face, he walked over to a panel and pressed a button. The grin vanished when nothing happened. He pressed it again and again.

Big Yellows yelled, "Stop that, fool!"

Little Yellows moved so quickly that I could not see it. Gray was instantly captured, and the other Grays were getting upset. Little Yellows walked over to Blue and dropped the Gray. Blue put one tentacle on the Gray and stood him up. "Don't do that again, Gray. It would have paralyzed the creature, and we would get nothing for hours."

Gray said, "Did you not notice? It did not work."

Blue looked at Green, and Green went over to the panel and checked all the gauges. It returned and said, "It worked but did not affect him."

Big Yellows asked, "If it worked, then why was I not harmed?"

Green looked shocked and returned to his equipment. He opened a panel and looked for any tampering but couldn't find any. He picked up a weapon-looking item—a long pole with a ball on the end—and placed it in the liquid in which I was floating. It did not give him the reading he was looking for. He disconnected a large cord from my tank and then from another and swapped them. Then he started up another panel.

I thought, *Darn, the power is back, and that panel is too far away. I was just barely able to mess with the close one. Well, I'll think of something. I need to keep my mouth shut for starters.*

Green took another reading on the tank and was happy. He said, "There is something wrong with the power coming from that panel. I changed to another panel, and everything is working correctly now. I think I know what the creature was doing earlier." He looked at me and said to one of the other Greens, "Take a reading on this tank every ten minutes. Between each reading, take the meter out and calibrate it before coming back in. We wouldn't want to give the creature a chance to tamper with the meter." To another Green, he said, "Troubleshoot that panel, and fix anything you find wrong. The creature caused the system to bypass the tank. Start there, and don't believe the readings on the gauges." He turned to me and said to Blue and Yellows, "He has learned how to run our equipment. He is a Red, and he is very dangerous. If he gets free, he could find a way to take over this ship."

Blue said, "Then don't allow him to get free. Continue with the probing. The longer we wait, the harder it will become to stop him."

Little Yellows took over and said to me, "You are a pest."

I said, "I try my best."

C H A P T E R   1 3

✦ ✦ ✦

SACRIFICES

At the planet Damien, one ship waited: the communication ship, ES *Maple*. She was one of six communication ships all named after trees. Her captain was upset about not being in the fighting and was even more upset with his orders to hide or run if attacked. However, the communication ships were not built for war and could not stand up to these new weapons the enemy apparently had.

The science officer said, "There is a ship coming in fast from quadrant six, sir. It appears to be one of our shark-class scout ships."

"Put her on screen, Lieutenant."

"Yes, sir."

As soon as the captain saw the ship, he yelled, "Rescue stations! Lieutenant, launch a shuttle to pull that fighter in."

Communications reported, "Her communications seem to be out, sir."

"Of course it's out, Ensign. It's a wonder she made it this far. Look at the scaring. She's banged up bad. Oh yes. She's seen fighting. I just hope she can slow down enough for us to attach and pull her brave crew in."

No sooner had he said that than the tiny ship's engines

stopped and shielding gave way. There was a minor flash of light and then an explosion, and the scout was gone.

The captain swore under his breath.

"Captain, there is a message tube headed our way."

"Reroute the shuttle to pick up that message tube, and bring it to me immediately. Something was important enough to cause that captain and crew to die to get us the information."

"Shuttle says they have it, sir. It's contaminated, sir. Highly radioactive."

"Tractor-beam it to the aft airlock."

"Where are you going, sir?"

"Lieutenant, you have the ship." The captain left the bridge.

At the aft airlock, the chief was waiting to cycle the air as he watched the deadly tube slowly move into the center. When it sat perfectly in the holder, the lieutenant said on the overhead, "It's in the airlock, Captain."

"Cycle the air, Chief."

The chief checked to ensure the door was locked manually and could not pop open when the pressures equalized. As he hit the button to cycle the atmosphere, the captain showed up, hastily donning a shield belt.

"Captain, you're not seriously considering going in there, are you?"

"Chief, glad you're here. Leave, but go to a ship's communication panel, take video of everything I hold up, and record what I read."

"Captain, you—"

"*Now*, Chief!"

The chief left, considering the captain was preparing to open the door.

Two rooms over, the chief stopped and flipped a switch on a panel. "I'm in place, Captain. Any chance of talking you out of this?"

He watched as the captain turned on the shield belt and opened the door. "You recording, Chief?"

"Every bit of it, Captain."

"Good. I don't feel a thing, so I think Dr. Anderson's shield belt is working."

"It has a warning that it wasn't tested against radiation, Captain. From what I hear, they won't allow him radioactive materials to play with."

The captain laughed. "Probably true, but it's being tested today. Okay. I'm walking over to the tube. I have it. Now to open it." The captain tried hard to unscrew the lid. He put all his effort into it, saying, "I wonder where they picked up radiation. There is none aboard any of the ships."

The lieutenant cut in. "In their hurry to get here, they must have run through the corona of some sun. It's the only thing I can think of."

"Can't be, as that would have removed the blast marks and left only the pits."

He placed the tube on his leg for more leverage and turned the lid with all his might. The lid turned and finally came off. Out popped a shielded black box. The captain instantly used his body to shield the box from the radiation and then backed out. After shutting the door, he did a complete scan of his shielded body, and there was no radiation detected. He checked the box and removed the data crystal; it was radiation-free also. "It worked, Chief. I'm clean. Open up."

Cheers were heard throughout the ship.

"On my way, Captain."

The captain walked over to a wall panel and placed the chip into the reader. "Lieutenant, download this information and have it ready for me to watch when I reach the bridge."

On the bridge, the captain and most of the crew watched the screens as the scout maneuvered frantically through the asteroid belt. They saw the quick turn, the destruction of the enemy ship, the decision to forgo days' worth of repairs and head straight for the nearest known ship. The crew of the scout did everything to hold her together. They were too far away from the rendezvous point. Environmental was out, and time was nearly out. They decided to sling around a black hole—that's where they picked up the radiation. The increased speed, however, gave them hope, and they prepared for the worse. The last thing on the screen was a fire starting in the engines and the tube being brought forward. Then all went blank as the black box was cut from the wall.

The captain sat back with a tear of pride for this brave crew that willingly sacrificed so much to get this information to fleet. "Communications, open up a wide channel to all ships in the fleet."

"Channel open on all bands and at full power, Captain."

The captain leaned forward and said, "This is the captain of the ES *Maple*. A ship just entered our space and exploded but not before sending the following in a message tube." He motioned for communications to play the message. When the message was completed, he said, "Report in. I want to know everyone who received that message."

The ES *Insight* echoed the message, and so did the *Hero* and the *Protectress*. Soon, confirmations were coming in from all quadrants.

✦

Little Yellows said, "Brave crew, little one."

I was crying but said, "Many are."

Gray said, "They deserve a decoration."

Blue said, "That kind of sacrifice only comes from

love—a love of family and country. And yes, they deserve their highest decoration."

I said, "They were posthumously awarded the Earth Federation Medal of Honor—our highest."

Green said solemnly, "Let's continue."

CHAPTER 14

✦ ✦ ✦

LOSSES

After their main weapons' weakness to attacks was found, the air battle was essentially over. There were little skirmishes here and there, but the enemy seemed to have vanished. Still, the war continued for months, as Admiral Penn had success after success in finding and destroying all flight capabilities. The specials became extremely handy in finding the Sycloyeds. They could quickly detect any running ships and determine if there was resistance on a planet that was fighting back against the Sycloyeds. Only a few planets had any resistance, and that was because their world had not been sanitized yet. The fleet landed troops on those worlds and joined in on the rebellion. With over ten thousand multinational troops on each world, the fleet took out the Sycloyeds quickly and efficiently. None could hide from the scanners and specials, when they paired up. Most of the specials were just kids and well protected from the fighting, but sadly, several still lost their lives. All told, 10 specials, 132 military personnel and eight ships were lost before it was over. Nearly all the dead were ground troops. Some died because of the Sycloyeds, and the rest fell to infections they picked up on new planets. Luckily, the fleet had the AD. Without it, we would have lost half the fleet to the microscopic bugs the army brought back with them. They were nearly all sick.

Admiral Penn sent a message to me, saying, "Bad thing about the ADs, Freddy—they do not allow for immunity to build up."

I sent an answer: "Easy fix, Admiral. Should take only a few days."

✦

Blue and Gray yelled at the same time, "I want that AD!"

Little Yellows giggled. "You have something to purchase your planet's life with."

I said, "You do not understand. You are still working under the assumption that you have won. You have not. You attacked like cowards, without warning, and from a now-protected blind spot. You have angered my species. Sadly, you have awakened and united the human spirit, and it is furious. I do not think I can talk my people out of their revenge."

Gray said, "Foolish little nothing human. We won that battle, and we will continue to win. No species has ever won against the might of our fleets. Now be still."

Little Yellows mumbled to Big Yellows, "There is always a first time."

I whispered to both, "It is those who think themselves invincible that are the danger to their species."

✦ ✦ ✦

PROTECTING HOME

The Sycloyeds must have found out where their new enemy came from, and that's why they disappeared from the fleet area. Ninety-six ships appeared only half a light-year out from Earth. It was the combined remainder of their fleets. Going by the pictures that the short- and long-range scanners provided, it was a very ragtag group—something of every type of ship that the Sycloyeds had. This included three of the planet sanitizers, or mother ships. They were directly behind five base ships, or carriers. The five base ships were overloaded with fighters.

I was in my shop, working on the AD problem, when the shop computer, who was scanning the system, detected the ships quickly moving in. The shuttles, moon base, and my small Mars installation picked them up also. The media picked them up shortly after we did. The ten shuttles were not going to keep this many away from Earth, not with each base ship having a thousand fighters. It was far too many for them to handle, and all our fighters were out with the fleet. We were spread out over thousands of light-years, and two days ago I'd sent the latest destroyer out to meet the fleet. Captain James came to me in the shop with a worried expression.

"Hi, Susan."

"Hello, Freddy. We seem to have a problem."

"I know."

"The world is in a panic, Freddy. The president is asking for help. Our ten shuttles can't stop all of those ships, and the fleet can't make it back here in time. They're on the way, but we don't expect the first ship for over five hours. We expect the Sycloyed fleet to be here in less than thirty minutes. People are panicking all over the world. You said you could protect us. Where's that miracle?"

"Susan, I can protect us several ways. Let's pick the combination that will work best."

"Go ahead."

"First, I can place a temporary shield over one-third of Earth. That should stop them from destroying us long enough for the fleet to arrive. The mother ships are slower than the others and will take more than five hours to reach a good firing position. However, two-thirds of Earth will most likely be destroyed, and the moon base and Mars installation would be vulnerable. The shuttles would need to protect the other two-thirds of Earth. The problem with that is that the Sycloyeds can take out the shuttles fairly quickly. All they need to do is gang up on each one. They know the tactic.

"Second, I can put up my new ship. Our shuttles cannot take out their mother ships, but she can. With her help, some of the shuttles could protect the moon and Mars installations while she takes out the bigger ships, and the shuttles can then do mop-up. It's not likely we'd get them all before they reached Earth. In addition, if any come to this side of the planet, I can destroy them with the MAGNA placements at this base. I estimate the chances of one of their bigger ships getting through at about 30 percent. Hundreds of the smaller ships will get through, and they could cause a considerable amount of damage. Besides, the shield won't hold long, stretched that thin."

"Freddy," she said tersely. "What are MAGNA placements?"

"MAGNA stands for Molecular Anti-Gravity Non-Alignment. It projects a field of gravity fluctuations so that every molecule in its path fluctuates separately between negative five hundred gravities and positive five hundred gravities. The molecules repel each other and fly apart. I'm adding the weapons to my new class of carrier. At this site, I have some adjusting to do, as I haven't corrected the distance on the beams yet. They still reach too far, and I don't want them to hit the moon. That would be a bad thing."

"Where are they?"

"Up there." I pointed to the ceiling. "Third and probably the best choice is this." I held up a small ball about the size of a baseball. "I can also put up two hundred of these."

She backed up quickly. Susan recalled the last ball I'd played with. When detonated, it took out a one-half light-year radius of space in all directions from point of impact. It's what I used to destroy the rock that was going to destroy Earth.

"Freddy, are those like the last ball you played with?"

"No way."

She calmed down. "Thank goodness."

"The last ball I played with was just a toy. This ball is considerably more sophisticated." She quickly stood up and seemed faint. I helped her sit down and said, "Susan, I was just getting you back for thinking I would develop another one of those balls. I told you I would not, and I keep my word. You know that."

"I'm sorry." She pointed to my little baseball and asked, "What do these do, then?"

Very sadly, I said, "They're designed to go up into space and lock onto anything I think of. When locked on, the transporter inside allows them to teleport into the heart of the object and explode into ten of these." I held up a marble-sized ball. "Each one will fly throughout the object, looking for the main power source, if any. When they find it, or after thirty seconds, they explode like a small thermo-nuclear device, or TND. My TND doesn't have fallout. No radiation. It takes out about one mile of space but leaves a lot of junk. The shuttles are going to have a wonderful time trying to clean up the mess. I was just debating sending the balls up when you walked in."

She smiled and said, "This I've got to see. Please send them up, Freddy."

I know I turned white at the thought of harming any creature, but Susan put a hand on my shoulder and said, "It has to be done."

I turned to the scanners and picked up a ball. I tossed it up, and it disappeared. I picked up another, looked at the screen, tossed the ball up, and it disappeared. I continued to do this and was on the sixteenth ball when one of the mother ships blew apart. By the time I tossed up the fortieth ball, there were no more enemies to destroy. The Sycloyeds must have thought it was some kind of invisible attack. They all swarmed together into several tight groups. Wrong tactic. The thirty-fifth through thirty-eighth balls took out all the rest. The last two balls I mentally detonated.

I started crying and turned to Susan, putting my arms around her and holding on. I was shaking. I had just destroyed a living creature—a lot of living creatures. I'd never felt so sad in all my life.

Susan understood and held me; calming me down and trying to help me get over this. I know she thought I was being silly; I picked up on her thoughts and let go of her. My heart was so sad that I turned away and asked her to leave. Before she left, I turned to her and said, "It's going to get out real soon that the Sycloyed fleet just blew up and that I'm a killer. They're going to find out anyway, so go ahead and tell them I did it. Tell the president first, as she'll need to calm the masses. Don't tell anyone how I did it. We may need that trick again, though I do have several other interesting ways to protect us. I need time to rethink what I'm doing here—why I'm inventing in the first place." She started to come back to me, but I motioned for her to go.

She wasn't gone more than a minute or two before Colleen came in with Kim. Kim is a special who is high in empathy. They sat down on each side of me and took my hands. I poured out my feelings without even wanting to. Kim is good at getting people to talk about their troubles. I even told them about missing Becky. Colleen is my best friend, and with her there to assist, I worked out my issues. It took a long time. I won't go through all that was said over the next three weeks, but I'm okay now.

Gray looked at Green. "Are our Reds that way? I have not had much dealing with Reds. There are so few of them. But this one seems strangely sad about protecting himself. I do not understand."

Green said, "Most of our Reds are exactly that way. It is one of the reasons that they do not invent some of the things you request. Some Greens are also that way. It is not a matter of protecting themselves. They do not like to see others harmed. Most Greens could not care less. I am one of the ones who cares."

Little Yellows said, "This creature does not like to harm anything. But he puts that aside to protect his species. He is blocking me from reading his thoughts at this time, as he is designing a weapon to fight against the undead. He believes that undead are an abomination to his God. Though he does not like doing so, he would destroy anything that is a potential threat to his people or world."

Gray asked, "Can you tap into that designing?"

Little Yellows said, "Yes, and every time I do, he stops and hides the information."

Gray said, "Be sneakier!"

Little Yellows was just about to slam him, but Blue grabbed him and lifted him up. Instantly, the other Grays pulled weapons; just as quickly, Big Yellows telekinetically removed them and stood between the Blue and the other Grays.

Blue said, "Gray, you go too far. First you question Yellows on doing her job, and then you threaten me."

Black walked back into the room. "Blue, allow me to straighten this one out."

Blue put the Gray down. "As you wish."

Black picked Gray up and walked over to the other Grays and started beating them with the body of the lead Gray. Shortly, they were all cowering. Black walked over to the tank and said to me, "We place Grays as our fighters for two reasons. They are the weaker, but they are the more aggressive and multiply quickly. They are tough little creatures, as you can see." He dropped the lead Gray, and the Gray scrambled to his feet and took his proper place. "However, the second reason is that we can control them, as we are stronger. It is not the same with your species. Your strongest is in your military, and they are trained to be that way." He paused before telling me, "Even a Black cannot destroy an undead. What makes you think you can?"

I said, "Because I can. I am working on the fourth way to do so now. The other three have already been sent to my people."

Black said, "You are under a delusion that your species will be alive to fight the undead."

I said, "You are under the delusion that you have won this war and that it is over."

Black stared at me long and hard before saying, "Green, continue."

C H A P T E R   1 6

✦ ✦ ✦

RUMORS

Susan came by when I was feeling better. "Freddy." She gave me a hug. "You're amazing. The whole world wants to hug you. Again, you saved us, and this time you saved several hundred worlds from a threat that was just as devastating as that rock. Now about those gun emplacements ..."

It figured she wouldn't forget about that. I spent several hours showing Susan some of my newest protections. She then told the rest of the team and set up training. Everything had to be run from my area of the shop, so I now had others in my workspace. Nothing seems to work out the way I first imagined it. I think I need to rethink my thinking. Of course, I do have another surprise or two.

With the whole team in my area, the new ship was now out for everyone to look at. The guesses about what it was were flying around base. In only one day, I heard the following:

"It's a super-cruiser just for Freddy's use. With it, he can destroy the fleet."

"Freddy's going to use it to elope with Becky when he's

old enough." (Nice thought, but she was still mad at me. Women hold grudges for the longest time.)

"It's a starship to take us to other galaxies." (Good guess but no.)

"It's a time machine. He can go so fast in it that he can outrun time." (I did the math; not going to happen. At least not yet.)

My favorite was the bad-boy theory. One of the team spread the story that I built the ship so that I could outrun the captain the next time I was in trouble and needed to be taken down a notch or two. That was a great possibility, but Susan hasn't had to smack me in two years. Not since just before the war began, and now that I'm fifteen, I don't think she will—at least I hope not. I nearly lost my lunch with laughter when I heard that one. Susan was not amused.

She came to me in my shop that afternoon. It was about two months after the war. "Freddy, where are you?"

Since my AD was completed and patented now, I spent most of my time in the new ship. It was taking me a lot longer than expected, but during the war I had to work on other issues. The ship was nearly completed, and that's where I was. "I'm in here, Captain," I said from engineering. I listened to her walk up the aft gangplank and head back to engineering with new exclamations of astonishment every several yards.

I had just finished putting in the controls for the new drive. This system gleamed. The entire ship was designed to make the average person, like me, feel like he had to walk quietly. You know that feeling you get when you're walking through a great museum or religious monument? That's the feeling I get every time I walk through this ship. Its design is very sleek, yet it's bigger than the carrier. The walls glow brightly with light and colors, so no other lighting is needed. There are only a few shadows. The power built into the walls will last for hundreds of years, and each individual section can be regulated for sleep.

The ship is laid out so that you can start at any point and get to any other point with the smallest effort. All connections run into hubs that use transporters to teleport you to any other hub you request, as long as you have the clearance to go there. I can go from the top-forward starboard side of the ship to the bottom-aft port side in only seconds, yet the ship is nearly four miles long. In case the transporters are down, there are standard moving shafts—one shaft for moving aft and one for moving forward, with several cross sections spaced at convenient points.

I have to say that this ship is my masterpiece. The drives in this ship look like large white funnels. In actuality, they are pure energy, concentrated so much that they pulsate and spin. To put it in a simple nonmathematical term, they're the opposite of black holes. I like to call them white vortexes, as they are so lightweight they generate negative gravity. The energy they give off creates a power that will allow for travel that will far exceed anything running.

Susan made it to engineering. I asked, "What's up, Susan?" She didn't answer. Her eyes were stuck on the drives.

"Ship's computer 'Susan,' please modulate the power shields to opaque."

A nice lower-range soprano voice said, "*Compliance, Freddy.*"

The shields around the vortexes changed, and the drives were hidden.

"*Is this the person I was named after?*"

"Yes."

"*Why?*"

"Because she is the only person that I consider smarter than I am and because she is beautiful, just like you."

With a smile in her voice, she said, *"Good reasons, Freddy. You've been around the team enough to understand the right things to say. She's coming awake. If this is the normal reaction to my drives, then I think I need to keep them out of sight most of the time."*

"Good idea."

Captain James came to her senses with a shake of her head. "Freddy, this is wonderful. It's the most fantastic vessel I've ever seen, or read, or thought of."

"Thank you, Capt. Susan James."

"You're welcome," Susan said, looking around.

"Capt. Susan James, meet Susan. She is the smartest computer in the known galaxy."

"Hello, Captain."

"Hello, ah, Susan. Freddy." She turned to me. "We'll talk about you using my name for your computer in a minute, but right now I need your help. I'm getting very tired of trying to squelch the rumors of what this ship is supposed to be for. The imagination of some people on this base is way out of control. Will you please tell me what you're building?"

I took the time to think on this by wiping my hands on a towel and heading out of the ship. Finally, I asked, "Just between the two of us?"

"No. I need to squelch the rumors before some of them strike fear in the wrong people, and they start causing problems. Have you heard the latest?"

"Probably, but go ahead anyway."

"'Poor Freddy has gone insane. After the war and after having to kill the enemy, he lost it. He just couldn't take destroying anyone. Not even the Sycloyeds. Now he's building a ship to leave us all. He's going to leave us because he can't stand being around all this fighting. He's going to take everything with him and destroy the fleet so we can never catch him.' I transferred the fool who made up that rumor. I wanted to have him skinned. People are thinking you're leaving us, and they're starting to panic. I'm expecting a call from the president any moment. This is starting to upset me a lot, and it's causing problems for the base. So spill it. What's it for?"

"Think, Susan. What is my priority?"

"Making up with Becky?"

"Well, I spent two days at the inn, and she still won't talk to me. Besides that."

"I would have to say the colonization of other planets, but you're not scheduled to start that for another two or three years. And besides, we have already started."

"Emergencies like war being the exception, what do we need to do before we put people down on a planet we are not sure of?" I asked

"Investigate it. I suppose you need to determine if it's safe. Ensure that there are no microorganisms that could spread to home. You were correct on that one, Freddy, and the president is grateful. You've told us several times, 'Keep it simple,' but ..." She paused, and I could sense an idea forming in her head. "Simple. Keep it simple, and do everything in order. You always preach this. It's the research ship, isn't it?"

"Yes." I had a big smile on my face. It changed to one of determination. "This ship and I"—I pointed to myself for increased emphasis—"will be going out to other planets sometime within the next year."

"Freddy, you really can't think that—"

"No, Susan! Due to the war, I lost the chance to be the first to set foot on another planet. I won't lose this chance. I am fifteen now. I expect I will be sixteen before I leave, but I'm going with her to the stars!" I crossed my arms and put on the most stubborn look I could manage.

She looked at me and said, "I can see that your mind

is made up on the subject. Perhaps we'll talk about it later, when you're a little more open-minded."

"Don't hold your breath. I don't care what the president says about my not taking chances. This is my ship! I built it! I paid for it! I'm going with it! And that's that!"

"I won't argue with you at this time, Freddy. Any idea how long before she's ready to go? What personnel will be needed?"

"She'll be ready for the finishing crew in about a month. They'll need about six months to get her ready for flight. Who will be going with me is still up in the air. I plan on inviting Dr. Landers and his team. Possibly Dr. Nguyen and his team also. I would expect that some of the SEAL team will come with us. I would also expect that some of the fleet would come with us. This ship is capable of protecting herself, but we don't really know what she may find out there. And"—I turned to the ship and placed a hand on the side—"she's very experimental. Everything is new. We need that escort to help us if anything goes wrong."

"She'll have an escort; I can promise you that. She's beautiful. Now change her name. Try Becky—that could get her to spend more time with you. You could have Becky christen it."

"Okay, Mother," I said in my best little-boy voice, which was difficult to do when my voice still had the tendency to crack at the worst possible moments. "I think that's a wonderful idea."

Susan grabbed me and rubbed the top of my head, laughing.

When we both calmed down, I said, "Susan, 'Becky' will be a good name for the ship, but for the computers, we don't have time in space to call out some long name to get the computers' attention. And it has to be one that's not too common. We're having problems with people who have the same name as the computer on my other ships. Admiral Penn says it gets confusing. Please, find me some naming criteria for my ships' computers."

"I'll put Colleen on it right away. We may be able to get your fan club to help. I'm sure they would love the chance."

"Speaking of my silly fan club, how's Julia Pears handling all that mail?" With hope, I asked, "Has she decided that I don't need a fan club anymore?"

"At first she had some real problems, trying to handle everything and still go to school. Her father started charging dues to belong, and now she has enough money to hire people to handle all the mail. It didn't work, Freddy. Your fan club has doubled since she started running it more professionally. Her father quit his job and is now in charge of mail and marketing. Her mother is going to personally answer some of the mail in a new magazine that's coming out next month."

"I hate to ask."

Susan smiled. "The name of the magazine is *Freddy's Folly*. And it's expected to have record sales for a magazine."

"It's got my name on it! Do I at least get some say on the contents?"

"Actually, your lawyers have insisted on editing it before print. You can edit it yourself if you want."

"No thanks! Can't we do something?" I asked with a whine.

"I knew you'd want to try, but if we put a stop to it, they would change the name to *Folly* and sell it without our edit."

"Darn."

"Julia would like to know if someone on the base could write a column about you and if you could write a column each month."

I was about to say "*no way*," but then it hit me. I smiled really big and said, "Yes, I'll write a column each month or each week, if she wants. You think I can put an apology to Becky in there?"

Susan looked at me skeptically. "The apology I understand, but why would you want to write a column, Freddy? What are you up to; you little sneak?"

I thought, *I wish she would stop looking at me as little. I'm nearly as tall as my father, and he made it all the way to five foot five.* With a smile, I said, "Nothing really, but the entire column will be in math. If they want to read it, they'll have to learn the math to decipher it. I've been looking for a way to get my ideas on math out to the public, and this may be a very good way. I'll start out simple, using only one principle. If that goes over well, I'll add another mathematical idea. At the end of the year, I'll have twelve ideas out to the general public. Do you think anyone will actually read my article?"

"Freddy, if you write it correctly—and we'll help—then yes, I do. I think many will count it the puzzle of the month. I warn you, though. If you do this, you may increase the circulation of the magazine considerably."

"If it gets the mathematical word out there, and people start using it and teaching it, then I've finally found a reason to have a fan club. Tell Julia that I said yes. I will write a column, and let her know that the first twenty people that answer the final question at the end of one year get a free trip on one of my ships and a walk on Mars—if they pass the inspections to qualify."

"Freddy, Julia is going to want to kiss you for this."

"Yuck! If she comes anywhere near me, shoot me before she gets the chance, please."

Susan hugged me, saying, "Thank you for the information. This will help a lot." Then she left. I went back to work in the drives.

✦

Blue asked, "Do we have this Becky person?"

Green said, "I wish. No, we do not have Becky or Julia. We had the entire Crain family, but after some tapping of their knowledge, we let them go. Bad mistake."

Gray said, "Yes, we could have used her to make this one give us the information we want."

I laughed. One of those "thank God it didn't happen" type of laughs.

Little Yellows said, "We do not think it would have worked."

Gray asked, "Why?"

"When you said it, he laughed at you."

Gray said, "He is easy to read. His emotions will always tell us the truth. Notice that he was completely serious when we talked about weapons."

Blue added, "And when he says that the war has just begun."

Gray said, "Yes. That worries me. I have taken special protections just in case. A Great Ship is on its way with one of our top admirals."

Black exclaimed, "You ordered a Great Ship to this tiny battle?"

Gray said, "Yes. If nothing else, it will strike fear in their hearts."

I said to Little Yellows, "Two statements: the enemy of my enemy is my friend; and the bigger they are, the harder they fall."

Little Yellows smiled and said, "Those are interesting statements. Try these two. First, never underestimate your enemy, and second, always underestimate your friends."

I laughed and said, "Freedom is not free; it is paid for by the blood of those who fight for it."

She said, "If we were all clear, there would be something else to separate us."

I said, "Ah, we have a similar saying. If we were all white, then our eyes would be on trial."

She said, "The sun sets only for love; the moons rise for lovers."

I was trying to keep my mind closed; she was getting too close. I kept this banter up for a while as Green continued.

CHAPTER 17

✦ ✦ ✦

PRANK

"Mother!' He calls me that just to irritate me." Susan paused for some time to think outside of Freddy's build area. "So Freddy wants us to keep Julia away from him. How interesting. Maybe I should invite her to stay the summer. No, I won't do that to him or to the girls on this base. I love that kid too much for that. Kid! More like young man and becoming more handsome every day. He may pay no attention to it, but the girls on this base sure do. If he starts wearing clothing that shows off that hard-muscle physique he's been developing with all the hard work and exercise, I'll have fights and jealous rages to contend with, in addition to everything else."

Susan left the build area and stopped in the new office building long enough to admire the new structure. Colleen had said she needed somewhere to do paperwork in the build area, and Freddy overheard her. The next day, several hundred robots were working on the issue. They completed the project in just three days—and it was amazingly beautiful. The office was set into the side of the mountain, with windows looking out into the build area on one side and shielded windows looking out on home base on the other. Susan walked up to the guard. He snapped to attention and gave a perfect salute.

"Good morning, Captain James."

She returned the salute. "Good morning"—Susan read his name tag—"Petty Officer Owens. Is Colleen in her office?" It rankled her that there were too many people on the base for her to remember all their names. Her irritated look was not lost on the petty officer, and he became nervous.

"Yes, ma'am. She just went in."

"Thank you. Carry on."

As Susan entered, she took the opportunity to look around. Smiling, she thought, *Perfect symmetry. I'll bet everything is within one-thousandth of an inch.* Each corner was rounded just a little to keep people from being cut on the perfect edges. The natural, highly polished rock colors stood out in a beauty that could not be duplicated. It was the same in the build area, but there were so many robots doing so many different things that she never noticed the beauty of the place. This was a quiet place to think—a peaceful place to contemplate. In the center was the most exquisite and spectacular water fountain ever designed. She walked past the fountain and ran a hand across it. The water was as smooth as glass. The fountain was suspended in the air several feet off the floor and continued up twenty feet. The dome-shaped ceiling was two hundred feet above that. The fountain received water from a source that could not be detected, even with scanners, and then the water simply disappeared. In four levels, it cascaded over sea creatures, outlining them in a white froth. Then the water became like glass again until it fell on the creature below it. The creatures were not really there, as you could put your hand through them and feel nothing but water. Yet every curve, whisker, hair, and movement was highly visible. The creatures moved around like they were playing on a beach. The engineers and scientists had studied the fountain but had no idea how Freddy did it. Freddy thought of everything to make this a great place to work, contemplate, or just relax. Susan got a little angry when she realized that Freddy never relaxed anymore. *Far too many demands*, she thought. *He really needs a long vacation.*

She walked into the foyer of Colleen's office and up to her door, giving it three light taps. Unlike the build areas, the acoustics here were very good, and knocking loudly would have startled Colleen.

"Come in, Captain." Colleen didn't have to speak above a whisper with the dot still following her.

Susan walked into a very nice room, fit for a little girl—all pastel pink—but Susan found it sickening. All the chairs were slightly too small for a grown-up. The desk was short and too small. There was a small canopy bed with pink lace and ruffles, and there were dolls all over the place.

"What happened, Colleen?"

"Freddy happened—that's what. I'd finally arranged this place how I liked it, and he changed it to this!" Colleen's tone indicated pure repugnance; Susan I could not blame her. Colleen continued, almost in tears because she was so mad. "I have no idea where the other furniture went, or I'd have it changed back right away."

"This furniture was supposed to go to the new dorm for specials. I'll bet there's a little girl there with your office furniture. I'm sure she'd love to exchange."

Colleen picked up the phone and called the dorms.

A girl answered. "Dorm two. This is Peggy. How may I help you, Chief Colleen McMasters?"

It always unnerved Colleen that they knew when she'd call. The phone hadn't even rung.

"I seem to be the proud owner of a little girl's room of furniture, and I hear you may have my office furniture."

The girl giggled. Colleen started to get angrier.

"Freddy is very good," said the girl. "We never caught him. We never even had a hint. You're in your office, so I'll send over a couple of kinetics to pick up that stuff, and then we'll reset your office to exactly the way it was."

Colleen said, "Thank you."

"Don't be mad at Freddy. He works so hard, and he worries about Becky. He hasn't had any rest in a long time, what with the war and all. We're protected and get schooling and playtime. He gets nothing except more work. Have you noticed that the longer he works, the more pranks he plays?"

"No. I never noticed that."

"Count it out. You'll see."

"Thanks."

"You're welcome."

After Colleen hung up the phone, Susan asked, "So is everything straightened out?"

"Yes, Captain. It's all fine. Peggy said that Freddy needs a vacation. That's the reason he's playing pranks again. He's overworked."

"Good. I was just thinking the same thing. Colleen, please get with the correct personnel, and set something up—two full weeks this time, with lots of rest. I want him back here in an emergency, so keep a shuttle ready to pick him up and bring him back, if necessary."

"I can't help feeling that we're rewarding him for playing his pranks, Captain."

"Freddy will not look at vacation as a reward, but make it a nice, slow cruise to see Alaska and the glaciers. And Colleen, don't tell Freddy, but invite Julia Pears and her family."

"He'll have me shot. I love it," she said with a big smile.

"I think he needs to get better acquainted with her and she with him."

"Playing matchmaker, Captain?"

"No. Not with that frilly little pest. Still, he needs a girlfriend. Someone who's smart, loves him, and won't let him step on her. It would be nice if Becky would forgive him for that Tammy issue, but that's out for a while. So to set him up with someone, we need him to slow down, force him to take a break, and think. Doing that in a romantic setting with a very lovely girl like Julia may just be what he needs to start him thinking about other girls. Besides, it's my turn to play one on him."

"I don't think he'll give up on Becky so easily, Captain. However, we'll set it up so that the guards know to leave Julia and Freddy alone. Still guarding with scanners but not showing themselves. I'll set it up for first-class cabins next to each other and the time that they need to spend together."

"They need to plan out that magazine."

"Perfect. I'll get right on it. School's out soon, and Julia will probably love the chance."

"Keep me informed, Chief." Susan left, knowing Colleen would make sure that Freddy paid for this last prank. Smiling, she pictured Freddy stuck on a slow ship, with Julia there to take pictures. She nearly tripped as she laughed at the thought.

✦

Green said, "They don't allow him enough rest time. It's been three years, by his time frame, since his last vacation. That is dangerous. If a Red becomes overworked, he could make mistakes. That would not be a good thing."

Gray said, "Even the military takes time off for fun and games. To work for so long is not healthy."

Blue said, "We take time off also, but this is different. He could take the time off but does not. Why?"

Green said, "He has too much to do. There are no others to take his place. They have lots of Greens, but I think this is their only Red."

Yellows said, "In their entire species, they have only one Red? We do not think so."

Little Yellows said, "He is not the only Red, but he is the top Red."

Gray took a step back, "We took their top Red. No wonder they are after us. I would trade all our Clears for our top Red."

Green smiled until Blue said, "Gray, you would trade all our Clears for a good drink."

Gray smiled. "Probably. Green, continue."

I said, "Gray should try our Kentucky whiskey. If you want an alcoholic drink, it is very strong."

Gray exclaimed, "Your species has alcohol?"

I smiled. "In thousands of different blends and types. Some aged and some not. It is a passion of many of our people, though I don't understand why."

Green said, "A Red would not."

Gray said, "Thousands, you say. Your species may have some redeeming qualities after all."

CHAPTER 18

✦ ✦ ✦

OVERHEARING

W hat Susan and Colleen didn't remember was that I have always monitored Susan when she was in the shop. From the first day that Susan was allowed in, she'd had a dot attached to her. She exchanged it for a clear dot right away, but I have always monitored her. She knows this. I love her dearly and don't want her harmed, so I always insist on monitoring her constantly. Now, Susan is so used to the dot that she forgets someone could be listening in. Her dot is a "command dot," so only another command dot could listen. I am the only other one with a command dot. Normally, I pay no attention, unless my dot warns me that something is about to happen. Then, I'll take action to protect Susan. I've saved her life several times but never told her. When she started talking to Colleen and said my name, it got my attention.

I drummed my fingers on my newest invention, thinking, *So Mother and Aunt Colleen are planning to play a prank on me. What should I do? I'd like a vacation. I'm tired, and I know it, but I don't want to be stuck on some slow-moving, glacier-watching ship for two weeks with Julia.*

With Becky, it would be nice. Then, I might even find a

way to slow the ship down further—but not with Julia. Yuck! That's boring, not restful. "Why does Mother think that I need to spend time with Julia, of all people?" I wondered aloud. "Matchmaking! I'm only fifteen. I'm too young for marriage! For goodness' sake, Julia likes to watch me blush! Susan puts up with her only because she's a weapon to use to keep me humble. In fact, I can feel Mother's dislike for her, and it's strong. It may be because Julia is a lot like the frilly little girls that Susan seems to dislike. That's possible. Susan may be prejudiced against frilly little girls. Goodness knows she's not frilly. Maybe it's not the girls. Maybe it's the frills. What I should do is go along with this, and be kind and nice to Julia. Lead her along and make sure reports get back to Susan that I'm falling in love with Julia. That would chap Susan's hide, and I'd bet she'd pull me off that ship as quick as possible. No, that's not fair to Julia. I may not get along with her, but that's no excuse to treat her badly, and I wouldn't want those reports getting back to Becky. So Susan has a problem with little-girl frills. So do I. Most boys would. Although, some of the older girls really look nice with a little lace and ruffles. Interesting. I've never seen Susan wear anything with lace. What if I went along with a vacation? Something less boring but still with Julia. Suppose I require that my mother comes along with me. Just the four of us—Julia and her mother, me and mine. In fact, I could insist that she dress appropriately so that she doesn't stand out. Julia's mom is very frilly. That would mean that Susan would have to dress frilly also." I smiled at my cleverness but quickly realized that plan wouldn't work—Susan would simply say no. What would Susan agree to? Something not frilly, at least for her. "Got it. Dot, contact Colleen."

"Hi, Freddy. How can I help you?"

"Aunt Colleen, please tell Susan that I overheard her conversation with you just now." Quickly, I added, "Remind her that it's not my fault that she did not request a private talk with you. She knows that I still monitor her when she's in the shop. I don't want to be blamed for this."

Colleen's mind was radiating surprise. She said, "Thank you for being nice enough to let us know. I suppose you're not going to allow us to send you on vacation. Are you?"

"Actually, I think it's a great idea but not the location or the method of travel. I have a few new toys that I'd like to try out, so I need some time in the field—say, camping in the mountains, by the ocean, or in the jungle. It won't take me very long to test my new equipment. Therefore, I'll have plenty of time to spend with Julia, planning my input to the magazine. I will allow Julia and her mother to participate, however, only if my mother comes too. If Susan won't go with me, then I go without Julia. I will need twelve volunteers to play military games. And Colleen, we need to be way away from everyone, as it would not be good to let the world know what these inventions are. It will take approximately two weeks in the woods. Not much for me to do once I set the volunteers to work. You think someone can teach me how to fish? If Susan agrees to go along, then I'll let her plan out the whole expedition. She can take whoever else she wants with us, as long as it includes twelve volunteers and her. At the end of the expedition we will need to go to Mars. If Susan agrees, then we can take Julia and her mother to Mars also. I should think they'd like that. Besides, once I test out my theories in the jungle, I want to test them on Mars."

"Freddy, I'm not sure that the captain will go for this."

I teleported into Aunt Colleen's office and said, "Just see if she can stop me." And then I teleported out. Colleen was on the phone to Susan before I could close out the conversation through the dots. The stuff was about to hit the fan. Time to hide.

I slammed my shields up and went into my hidden office. Everyone knew the entrance but they had no idea what's back there, and Susan does not have access. In fact, the dot would warn her that entering the area would be extremely dangerous. That was because I told the shop computer not to give access to anyone, especially Captain James. It was also because my next project was there and in its start-up cycle. It was probably the most dangerous thing I'd ever attempted. Besides, I wanted it to be a surprise.

I was right. Susan came looking for me right away, and she wasn't alone. She had three of the specials with her. I told the shop computer that I didn't want to be disturbed and continued working on my project. I heard the shop tell her that entrance into this area is restricted. She tried to override that, but the shop computer told her that I was busy working on something that was important.

"If Freddy is distracted at this point, it could kill him."

This was true, as I had purposefully started working in that area of the project. Shop was programmed never to lie but getting around that was easy, if needed. Just do what you want the shop to report. I was really in it deeply now, so I had to pay attention to what I was doing and stop thinking about how mad Susan might be. Time was getting short, and my best and most dangerous project to date had to become reality in just a few short hours—or all would be lost.

✦

Green said, "He is working on a grand project. I am curious as to what it might be."

Black said, "We would never allow a Red to work alone. They are watched and closely monitored. Do you remember, Green, the issues one of your precious Reds created when she tried to move an asteroid into orbit around the home world?"

Green cringed. "That was hundreds of years ago. We have done great things since then."

Black smiled. "Yes, because you are watched and not allowed to be on your own."

Blue said, "All the colors have created issues in the past."

A Purple in the corner whispered to another, "And we end up cleaning the mess they make."

They all looked at the Purple.

Gray said, "Unless the mess they make puts us into war—like building machines that think."

Green said, "Machines have had the ability to think for a thousand years. It's when we made them sentient that the trouble started, and we did that at the request of the Grays for better fighting machines."

I mumbled, "Fools."

Little Yellows whispered to me, "We agree with you on this one." Louder, they said, "Green, you need to continue."

C H A P T E R   1 9

✦ ✦ ✦

SAFETY

Susan exclaimed, "That little pest! He's doing this on purpose! He knew I'd be coming after him to find out what he's planning and how he can teleport in and out of places."

One of the specials, Andy Roberts, said, "Captain, I can feel him, and he's really working hard on a project of some sort. I can't tell what the project is, as his shields are up, but it's something important and very dangerous. I can feel his worry."

Another. Diana Nickels, pulled on Susan's sleeve and said, "He always watches you when you're in the shop area. You know that. I can feel it. It's not his fault that you forgot. Besides, you should want to hug him for warning you that he overheard your conversation. Why are you mad and thinking he was spying?"

The other special, little seven-year-old Kay Brown, giggled and said, "He wasn't spying. He loves you. You're his mommy. He protects you."

Bending down to her level and rubbing her head, Susan said in a nonaccusing tone, "I'm astonished that the three of you can pick up so much without entering my mind." She stood up and thought for a second. *The specials all adopted Freddy's stance that you don't spy on someone's thoughts unless you think that person is pulling something bad. So they're not reading my mind. How do they know all that information? Think, think, girl! Wait a minute.*

"Shop."

"*Yes, Susan?*"

"How many times has Freddy actually kept me from harm while here in the shop areas?"

"*Twenty-three times to date, but only four would have resulted in your death.*"

Susan's face turned white, and she hoped it would quickly turn too red. Showing embarrassment was far better than fear, but there was no fooling these kids. One grabbed Susan's knee; the other two put their arms around her waist. All said things like, "Don't worry. You'll be all right," and "Freddy won't let you get hurt. He protects everyone." Now Susan was embarrassed. She quietly but firmly said, "Please let me go," which they quickly did.

"Now, how can we get Freddy to come out so that I can talk to him?"

Diana said, "Right now, that would be a bad idea, Captain. Freddy is really working in an area that is highly dangerous."

"Very well. He'll have to come out sometime."

"Why?"

Susan had to think about that one. *He probably has a ship in there so he has a place to eat, sleep, clean up, get fresh clothes, and communicate with the world. He has no reason to come out.*

"Shop."

"*Yes, Captain James.*"

"When Freddy is not busy doing something dangerous, please tell him that I am no longer angry with him. Tell him that I want to give him a hug for protecting me and that

I want to talk to him about some things. Let him know I approve of his vacation idea, as long as he gets to relax most of the time, as he suggested he would. Tell him that Cooky is making a chocolate cake with chocolate butter frosting for one of the team, and he should be present for the cutting. We'll be cutting it tonight at 1900 hours."

"I will pass the information on as quickly as possible. I expect to be able to inform him in about two hours. Knowing Freddy, he is going to ask for whom the cake is intended."

"Access all team records. Is there anyone with a birthday this month?"

"Forty-two personnel have birthdays this month, and eighteen are on the base at this time. One has a birthday today."

"Really? Who?"

"Katie Swanson."

"Perfect. If Freddy asks, tell him that we have started a new tradition. Each month, everyone will quit working long enough to celebrate the birthdays for that month by getting together and sharing a cake."

"He'll love that. You know how he feels about Katie. Besides, chocolate butter frosting is his favorite."

"I know. Thanks, Shop."

Little Kay Brown looked up and tugged on Susan's pants. "Are we really going to have chocolate cake tonight?"

"Yes, we are. Shop?"

"I know; tell Cooky what's going on so she can start making the cake. It will need to be a big one. She's going to be upset at the short notice."

"I'll handle her temper. You just tell her. Thank you."

"You're welcome."

Kay took off skipping and yelling in delight, "Cake! We're going to have cake!"

Both the others turned to leave also. Diana Nickels said, "You'd think she doesn't get dessert every night."

Andy said, "I know. I've never eaten better. But still, sharing cake with the entire team will be a lot of fun."

Susan decided that maybe this idea was a good one. *Sometimes I stumble onto the best ideas out of pure need*, she thought. This time, the need was to get Freddy out of his rabbit hole. With it being Katie's birthday, the chances were 100 percent that he'd be there.

Susan headed out to the new ship. *How am I going to talk Freddy into staying on Earth? It's not fair that he can't go into space, but he is the only one who can run this shop.*

"Shop."

"Yes, Captain?"

"How many times has Freddy saved the lives of people, including me, while working on his projects?"

"One hundred six times."

That stopped Susan dead in her tracks. "That's not acceptable! Shop, can you give me a report on every safety issue in which Freddy had to get involved?"

"Yes, that would be 721 issues."

"But you said 106!"

"That was 'save lives' only."

"Please break everything down into categories, and chart them from the most common to the least common."

"Completed."

"Send it to my console as a file labeled Safety Problem."

"Completed."

"Thank you."

"You're welcome, Captain."

Susan stared at the door to Freddy's new private area, wondering, *How much time has been lost because Freddy has had to monitor and protect all these people? For goodness' sake. It's my job to protect, and I'm not doing my job; he is.* Aloud, she said, "Thank you, Freddy. I promise I'll do better."

She left to talk with the cook. When she entered the

house, Cooky was just heading back into the kitchen, as happy as a lark.

"Hi, Cooky. Sorry for the short notice."

"Perfectly all right. Making a large cake is nothing. Just don't surprise me with presidential visits at the last minute anymore. Seven-course meals need to be planned out, you know." She continued into the kitchen, humming a song.

"Well, at least that's one less worry." Susan went into her office and opened the file marked Safety Problem. As soon as she started reading, she could see that they were in deep trouble. If OSHA—the federal Occupational Safety and Health Association—were to audit them right now they'd shut them down. Susan wasn't a safety expert, so she called Chief Peters into her office.

"You called, ma'am?"

"Yes. Take a look at this, and tell me what you think."

He came around the desk and read some of the material. With a look of pure irritation, he asked in a snippy tone, "What are you doing with this? This should have come through my desk!"

"I found out about it when I was in the shop, so I had the information sent to me directly. And watch your tone!"

Without looking up, he said, "We need to call Washington and get some experts down here immediately. I am so sorry. I never had a clue from the papers crossing my desk."

"You know, Chief, not everything is on paper or in that computer of yours."

He gave Susan a look that said she was being sacrilegious, and then he sent the file to his computer. "I'll have Environmental Safety and Health personnel here within the week! This has to stop!" As he was leaving, he mumbled as he wrote in his notepad. "We'll need safety identification and development training, monitoring, new person introduction, required shop access training, hazardous material and waste training and regulations, procedures for everything ..."

Once he was out the door, Susan could no longer hear him prattle, but the smile on his face said she'd given him his Christmas presents for the next two years.

"Home, please tell Shop to send any additional information on safety issues to Chief Peters."

"Captain, Shop has an emergency."

"Patch her through."

"Captain James, I need you immediately. Please come to the shop, and bring Stacy Michaels and Dr. Landers."

"Very well, Shop. I'm on my way." Susan quickly left, while telling Home to contact Stacy and Dr. Landers and have them meet her at the shop entrance immediately. When she realized who Stacy was, a special in healing, she started running. Stacy met Susan at the entrance, and Dr. Landers was close behind her.

"What's up, Captain?"

"I don't know, Stacy."

"Is Freddy all right?"

"I don't know. Shop wants the three of us—and now." They entered the shop and headed toward Freddy's area on a run.

"Captain, I have dispatched clear dots to each of you, as I don't want anyone else to hear what I am about to say."

"Go ahead."

"Thank you. Captain. Freddy received your message and was very happy, but in his enthusiasm, he slipped and hit his head on his new project."

Susan started to panic even more, but Shop said, "Relax, Captain. Freddy is not in any danger. He is doing fine, but he did hit his head rather hard. He is lying on the floor of his new project, unconscious. He is bleeding a little but not enough to be worried about it. I scanned him and can see that the injury is minor. However, unless someone goes in and wakes him soon, he may miss dinner and the cake cutting. That would be sad."

"Shop, anyone could have handled this. What's the matter?"

"Freddy's newest project is very dangerous, Captain, and I want it stopped."

That comment caused Susan to break into a run. She realized that the shop computer was doing something against its programming. "Shop, how are you getting around your programming to do this?"

"I cannot reprogram my ten top requirements, but I can reprogram myself in order to fulfill them."

Susan relaxed a little. Shop's top ten requirements all had something to do with protecting Freddy, personnel on the base, and the base, including itself. So the shop computer was still under control. "Very well. Why?"

"I had to reprogram myself in order to stop Freddy from destroying himself and possibly the world. I need you to talk him into stopping this project, at least until he has thought it through and has a much safer place to attempt the act."

"What is he doing?"

"I can't tell you that. However, I can tell you that he is hurt and that someone has to go rescue him. I think whoever rescues him may accidentally find out what he's doing. I can also tell you that you have only twenty-three minutes."

The three moved fast toward Freddy's private shop. "I understand, Shop. I will look into it, but you know how Freddy is."

"Don't I!"

Susan thought that sounded far too human—but they had arrived, so she said, "Shop, please open the door." She expected a click or something, but instead, the three of them were teleported through the wall.

"*There is no door, Captain. The door you've seen from the shop is just a decoy.*"

"This place is huge. Where are we?"

"*You're six hundred feet below the shop proper. Freddy calls this 'the retreat.' Please follow the small blue ball of light to the project area. It will lead you directly to Freddy. Wake him quickly.*"

"Thanks, Shop."

"*I wish I could say I was doing this for you, Captain, but in truth, I'm doing it to save the human race from Freddy's new toy. I don't understand it, and what scares me most is that Freddy doesn't understand major parts of it either.*"

"*Freddy* doesn't understand what he's doing?"

"*No. He told me so himself as he was giving me a message for the fleet to hold, in case anything went wrong.*"

"Please play back that message."

"*I cannot.*"

"Then play back the conversation about the message."

"*Very good, Captain. You're learning. 'Shop, I have no idea if this is going to work. If it does, I have no idea if I can actually contain it. I think I can, but if I can't, then send this message off to the fleet and then evacuate the entire base. If the fleet cannot destroy it, they may need to evacuate the rest of the planet.'*"

"That's not good." Susan was in the build area of the retreat now, and the equipment she saw caused her to lose her breath. *It's easy to see that the pest is building equipment for the army.* They stopped in front of a large circular structure with a sign: COLOSSUS.

"*He's inside approximately 128.2 meters to the right.*"

There was no door, and Susan was not sure how to enter, but Dr. Landers and Stacy dashed through a glowing, clear-liquid panel about ten feet tall and twenty wide. Susan headed in, and although the liquid formed around her, she did not get wet. In only two long steps, she was on the other side and running to catch up with Dr. Landers and Stacy. The path ahead of them was small, and they had to go single file for nearly fifty yards before it widened to ten feet. The walls, floor, and ceiling were covered in stainless-steel panels and equipment, making it look like they were standing inside the belly of a monstrous robot. They headed to the right. As they passed row after row of equipment, Susan saw signs that looked like whirlpools. When they reached Freddy, he was lying at an angle, up against equipment and across several tools, like a cat sleeping half across a fireplace hearth. The position looked painful. Dr. Landers and Stacy moved him to a clear space on the floor. Stacy checked him.

"Captain, he'll be all right. I can heal this easily."

"Don't do it yet. Dr. Landers, can you determine what Freddy is trying to build here?"

"I'll try." He got up and started going through the controls and looking at Freddy's notes as he moved down the row of equipment. They all started looking around. This was not like Freddy's other projects. This project was built to last forever; it was stationary and built in a way that made it feel heavy and extremely well protected.

Susan asked, "Shop, what kind of power is running this equipment?"

"*I don't know. It's something new, and I don't understand it.*"

"Freddy didn't talk about it?"

"*Constantly, but I can't keep up with his math. No known computer can.*"

Dr. Lander's eyes opened to the size of moons, and he looked like he wanted to run from this place.

"Captain, I think we need to leave. We need to leave now and send a crew in here to dismantle this unit. All of it."

"What is he building, Doctor?"

"A micro black hole—and he's almost finished."

"*What?*"

"He's attempting to build a black hole."

"Why?"

"I haven't the slightest. Can we leave now?"

Susan asked, "Shop, can you remove all power from this unit?"

"No. That has to be done at the power source."

"Where's that?"

"Two hundred feet straight down, in engineering. I would not suggest you attempt it. Doing so may cause a catastrophic reaction. The power source has the ability to power an impregnable shield that would surround the entire solar system. That much I understood. Freddy was thinking about changing the unit into something of that sort. He said it wouldn't take much. Right now, the system is nearly fully powered, and it's counting down. You have about eleven minutes."

"Can you teleport the four of us and his notes down to engineering?"

"That I can do."

"Please do so immediately." Susan then turned to Stacy, saying, "Please heal the little pest."

With a trembling voice, Stacy asked, "Captain, when Freddy wakes, he can teleport all of us right out of his shop. How are you going to stop him?"

"You just wake him up."

"That's going to take a few minutes."

"Stacy, we don't have a few minutes." The place suddenly changed, and they were on a narrow platform covered with equipment on one side and with a deep, circular cavern at least a hundred yards across. The cavern was completely smooth on all sides and straight down. They looked around for signs or something that gave a way to stop the unit. "Shop, what is that pit for."

"Captain, his power source derives directly from the planet core. He's tapping off Earth's energy."

"How deep does this pit go?"

"To the center core, Captain. Only the power in this room keeps the shields running strong enough to hold the power and liquid in the core from escaping. The pressure down in the hole is beyond what I can measure. I told him that I thought he was making a mistake, but he assured me he could close it just as easily as he opened it. Seven minutes, Captain. Six fifty-nine. Six fifty-eight. Six fifty-seven."

"Stacy, how's Freddy?"

"Still out of it."

"Six fifty-one."

Freddy started coming around. "Where ... where am I?" Then his eyes focused. "What? Why? How?"

"Six forty-five."

Susan took hold of Freddy and gave him just enough of a shake to clear his head. "Freddy, listen to me. Stop the countdown. Stop it now!"

"Six thirty-one."

"Captain James, you shouldn't be here. Please leave my retreat." He looked over and saw Dr. Landers and Stacy. "The two of you also. Stacy, did you fix my head?"

"Five fifty-six."

"Yes."

Freddy smiled and said, "Thanks. Why are you so afraid?"

"Five forty-three."

Stacy yelled, "A black hole, Freddy! You're building a black hole right below where I work and sleep!" She slapped him. Susan was shocked, and so was Freddy.

"Five twelve."

He got up with tears in his eyes, turned around, and walked to a console and started working.

"Four fifty-four. Four fifty-three. Four fifty-two."

Susan walked up to him and said, "Freddy, don't be angry. Before you make a black hole, we need to have a long talk."

"Three fifty-eight."

"Captain, if you want me to stop the black hole from forming, then I would suggest you let me be."

Susan quickly backed away.

"Two eighteen."

Freddy continued to press buttons and type into a console. He typed so fast that his hands were a blur. Then he disappeared.

"One forty-seven."

Dr. Landers yelled, "Over there!" He pointed to the opposite side of the hole. Freddy was there, working at a console. What was worse, however, was that the pit was moving.

"Thirty-three, thirty-two, thirty-one, thirty."

In the pit was a moving energy, and it was building up. A small explosion was seen in the center, and the movement became circular and picked up speed. After another explosion in the center, the speed was fast enough that Susan could feel the pull.

"Twenty, nineteen, eighteen."

Susan yelled, "Get back! Get away from the edge, and hold onto something!" Stacy and Dr. Landers dashed to the console and grabbed hold. Susan beat them there. The pull was getting stronger.

"Four, three."

A large explosion sent them to their knees. The pull stopped, and Susan looked up. The pit was gone—closed up—and the floor was clean. Freddy was stomping across the new floor, and he did not look happy.

"Captain James! If I could have sent the three of you out of here, I would have, but the energy fluctuations were too great for me to transport you without possibly leaving you in the astral plane forever. Helping me is one thing— and thank you very much—but why did you just *ruin* my project? It will take me months to set that all back up and fifty years for Earth to be aligned with the pools at the exact angle to the sun correctly again!" Turning to Stacy, he added, "And why did you slap me? For goodness' sake! What did I do now?"

Stacy yelled at him, "You tried to build a black hole right under my feet! That's what you did! How dare you! That's the most dangerous thing I've ever heard of! How can you do such a thing to me? I should tell all the specials what you almost did to them! You could have killed us all!"

Stacy was in tears, and Freddy was in shock. Then he seemed to come out of it as he turned and looked away. "Shop!"

"*Yes, Freddy.*"

"What did you tell them?"

The shop repeated everything that was said since Freddy's accident.

Freddy sat down in the middle of the new floor. He was in tears. "Shop, next time tell me if you're worried, and we'll talk about it. And if you still think I'm doing something dangerous, then ask Susan to talk to me. Don't let it escalate to a point where people get mad at me." He looked up with a sad expression and added; "Don't tell Susan what I'm doing, just that she needs to have a talk with me. I trust her."

"*Confirmed.*"

Susan sat down next to him and took him in her arms. "That's it, Freddy. No more games. No more places where you can build all by yourself. You can have a private office in the new office building where you can invent, but no build areas without supervision."

"But—"

"No, Freddy. I have to report this to the president, and she is not going to be happy. You stepped way over the line this time. I'll need to let her know we stopped you and that we are taking measures to ensure it never happens again. You could have killed us all and destroyed the planet and the human race. Private playtime is over."

"I'm sorry, Susan, but I can't allow that." Susan was shocked and starting to get a little angry, but before she could say anything, Freddy said, "No, don't. Not now. We're too emotional at this time. Let's talk about it tomorrow when I've calmed down. Right now, I'm confused and too mad to talk about anything rationally. Shop, how much time went by outside?"

Dr. Landers said, "Freddy, it's only been thirty minutes at most."

"Four hours and twenty-eight minutes, Freddy."

Freddy turned and looked at everyone. "The micro black hole would have worked, Dr. Landers. It would have supplied enough power to fulfill the world's needs for ten thousand years. No more pollutants, no more hazardous waste, and no more worry of attack. However, it has side effects, like time distortion, and that's what I was worried about. Not hurting people. Just displacing some of the workers that we would need down here in time a little. A few days at most. Now, I can't do it again for fifty years. I forgot about that message. I should have canceled it. I felt so bad about what I was doing that I stopped and rethought the entire process. I assure you I would not have continued if I didn't know what I was doing or if I might actually have harmed someone. Susan, you know me better!"

Dr. Landers said, "Sorry, Freddy, but next time talk to us. The entire world would have been against you on this one. They're a people made up of fears, Freddy. A black hole, no matter how small, is a fear that would have caused panic and riots. Its political effects could have resulted in war. In the future, when we are comfortable with it, perhaps we can try it out on one of the other planets in a different solar system and beam the energy where we want it. Until then, I would have to say no black holes, my boy. Not here. Not where I live."

"Well, it's too late for here anyway, sir. I'm a little tired and a lot hungry. Can we eat now?"

Susan couldn't help but hug him. "I'm sorry also," she said. "However, this is not over, sweetheart. We will talk about it first thing in the morning—before you go into the shop or anywhere else. We'll also talk about the trip. I want to know what you have planned." She got up and pulled Freddy up with her.

"Susan, you know better. I'm not about to give away my surprise until I'm good and ready. We can talk about it all you want, but the chances are really slim." He turned to the computer. "Shop, please engage backup power. Power up the transporter, and teleport us out of my retreat."

"Compliance."

Instantly, they were on the outside of the fake door. Shop whispered to Susan, *"Thank you, Captain James."*

"You're welcome, Shop. Please do exactly what Freddy stated and lock in that order to report to me so that no one, not even Freddy, can change it."

"Completed."

"Thank you."

✦

Blue looked at Green. "I thought that making a black hole to supply power was impossible. We asked the Reds to work on it, and they said it could not be done."

Gray asked, "What about this white hole he said he has for his research ship? That sounds powerful. And where is that research ship?"

Green said, "I was on the team that worked on the math

for the black hole. What we said was, 'With our current knowledge we cannot create a black hole.' We simply do not have the ability at this time."

I snickered.

Big Yellows said to me, "Quiet, unless you want to supply us with the knowledge."

I said, "Fat chance."

Gray asked, "Can we recreate this white vortex?"

Green said, "I do not think so."

Black said, "We will find this research ship of his. We will have this new technology."

I said, "Do not worry. She and her six twins will find you. But they are old technology. You should be worried about my recent creations."

Black said, "You can stop, child of Earth. We do not believe you."

I smiled and nonchalantly said, "Okay."

Yellows said, "Please, Green, continue."

CHAPTER 20

✦ ✦ ✦

ASSASSINS

This has been a bad day, I thought. *They ruined my project, and I can't blame them. I should have been better at communicating. My fault.*

Even though I'm tired, dinner and the cake cutting went very well. Several specials came up to me during the cake cutting and wanted to talk, and I actually enjoyed myself.

After singing "Happy Birthday" to all the appropriate people, a little girl named Samantha came up to me. She had her hands on her hips like she was really mad.

She said, "Freddy Anderson, you messed up my room. Putting all that adult stuff in there was not nice. If you want to play with your big sisters, you leave me out of it, or I'll tell my mommy."

She stomped on my toe and then stormed off, leaving me hopping on one foot and holding the other. Everyone was laughing at the sight except one woman. I stopped my jumping around and touched her open mind. She was upset that she had let that little girl attack me, and she was debating on taking the girl out. She considered the specials as "dangerous."

I became as serious as possible. Susan saw and said,

"Now, Freddy, you brought that on yourself. She had every right to confront you about the prank you played on her and Colleen."

"I agree with that Susan, but I don't agree with a person who is harmful to specials."

Katie was there, eating her cake, and she looked up, asking, "Who, Freddy?"

"The lady over there in uniform. Looks like one of the marines. Very short dark hair, jaw like a brick, and tall. She towers over the people next to her. She was thinking about taking out Samantha, as she considers specials—including me—as dangerous. She considered what Samantha did as an attack on me. However"—I paused, thinking—"she believes that it makes no difference, as I'm about to die."

Katie instantly went into action, and the team surrounded me. She made a small hand signal and pointed. The tall marine suddenly collapsed to the ground after being stunned by one of my disintegrating pistols. Six team members went to her—three navy SEALs and three marines. When they reached the woman, I heard Susan say in a very nasty tone, "Sorry, but you're being replaced. Katie, take Freddy out of here. Margaret, have this one investigated before she's removed. I want to know how she made it this far and what her plans were."

"Freddy, *duck!*"

Because of the warning, I teleported myself into my bedroom, just as I heard a shot ring out. I quickly checked myself, and I was all right. The shot had missed. The problem was that the shooter was in my bedroom. He turned and fired. I instantly put up a psychic shield, and the bullets that were coming pinged off the bubble that surrounded me. I then quickly tried to mind-freeze the shooter. Instead, he disappeared.

"Home, where did he go? And is anyone harmed?"

"He is outside the shop door. He knocked out the guard. He's trying to get inside. The bullet missed everyone."

"Thanks." I ran to my transporting portal. "Shop."

"Freddy, I have an intruder."

"Release a black dot."

"Working. Completed."

"Now open a door to my private shop."

"Opened."

I stepped into my secret shop and ran to my research suits. "Shop, block all use of psychic energies."

"That will leave you helpless, and he has a gun, Freddy."

"Understood, but I can't catch him when he can teleport at will."

"Completed."

"Shop, where is he headed?"

"Toward the small ships."

"Lock down all ships, and shield security A1. Anyone in that area?"

"I've already evacuated them."

"Where's the black dot?"

"He destroyed it before it got near him. He has a weapon that dissipates energy. Security in place and holding. He looks angry that he can't use his abilities."

"Great, just great. No sense releasing another black dot if he has the ability to destroy it."

"I can take him out with the lasers."

"And have nothing left of him to investigate? No thanks." I quickly climbed into one of my new research suits and powered up. I turned on the shields and checked the visual indicators to ensure that everything was working. "Shop, where is he now?"

"He is at the main entrance to this area. He is trying to force open the fake door."

"Perfect. Teleport me twenty feet past him and facing

him." The area disappeared, and I was suddenly standing in the shop proper. I was facing the intruder, and he was busy affixing some type of device to the fake door. I took a second to pick a weapon from the belt, and then I pointed it and fired. He collapsed. "Shop, scan the intruder, and ensure he is knocked out."

"*Scanning. All body functions show that he is fully unconscious.*"

"Great." I walked up to the intruder and touched him. "Shop, any change?"

"*No. He's still unconscious.*"

"Allow psychic powers again."

"*Completed.*"

The man shot me and disappeared. The bullet bounced off my shield but knocked me back two steps. (*Note to self: I need to work on kinetic energy absorption for this suit.*) I followed the intruder and teleported to the outside. When I reached the place where he'd exited from the shop, Patricia Henderson hit me hard enough to knock me to the ground, even with my shield on. She shattered the bones in her hand by doing it.

The intruder was lying on the ground. Patricia saw him emerge, and her training kicked in. She hit him hard, almost before he finished teleporting. I went to him and touched his head. I found the spot in his brain where special talents like his develop, and I damaged it. I had harmed a human. I was mad and sad at the same time. I turned to Patricia to fix her hand while talking to Shop.

"Shop, how did he get through your psychic shielding?"

"*Using his energy disrupter.*"

I was finishing repairing Patricia's hand by the time the rest of the team reached us. I said, "Hi, Susan."

"Freddy, what happened? Henderson, report!"

Patricia came to attention. "I took up watch at this

point, as per plan C, Captain. When this"—she kicked the intruder—"man emerged, I took him out. Then Freddy emerged, and I hit him before I could stop myself. I think I shattered my hand on Freddy. He's fixed it."

I asked, "How are the guards, Susan?"

"Both will be fine, Freddy. They were knocked out, but two of the medical specials are working on them. Please explain what you did, and why are you crying, sweetheart?"

"I'm crying because I'm extremely upset." I reported to her exactly what had happened and told her that the device was still attached to my fake door. "Susan, I need to remove it before someone gets hurt."

She took hold of me and gave me a hug. "That was very brave, Freddy. We'll have one of the others remove it with a shield box. I want to speak with you."

"Very well, Captain." I picked up the energy disrupter from the ground and then started taking off my suit. "I need a volunteer to remove that bomb. They can use my shielded environmental suit to do so, and they won't get harmed."

Susan ordered, "Chief Darnel, take care of that bomb or whatever it is, and give me a full report. Use the suit, and if we don't need the bomb then destroy it."

I showed Summer Darnel how to use my new suit, and she took off to remove the bomb.

"Shop and Home!"

"Yes, Freddy."

"Yes, Freddy."

"Please scan this weapon."

"Working. Completed."

"Completed."

"Please scan all areas within a fifteen-mile radius of home. Include all areas in home and the shop. I want an immediate report if any other weapons even remotely like this are found. Scan not just type but also power system, possible different styles, and material makeup. Start at home and work your way out."

"*Compliance.*"

"*Compliance. Freddy, there is another weapon in the room that Marine Sergeant Taylor Reynolds stayed in.*"

Susan made a quick movement, and two of the team peeled off, heading toward the small housing units.

"Susan, please stop those two!" I called out, and she did. "The room needs to be guarded, and no one is to enter until a special walks through and tells us who has visited that room." Susan sent them back out.

Home reported, "*Both Shop and I have completed all scans and found no other devices.*"

"Thank you."

"*You're welcome, Freddy. Shop suggests that she be given permission to fry the next one who illegally enters her areas.*"

"That's up to the captain."

Susan said, "Permission granted."

Shop said, "*Thank you, Captain James.*"

I looked up at Susan and said, "Captain, I want to know who he is working for or what country he is from, so please bring him with us."

"He's dangerous, Freddy. I don't think he should be around you."

"Captain, I just told you that I destroyed the part of his brain that allowed him to use his special abilities. He's not a special anymore." I started to walk toward the main house, but I could sense the fear from some of the other specials. They weren't afraid of the intruder. They were afraid of my removing their abilities. "Just a second, Susan."

With tears running down my cheeks, I turned to several specials and said, "Though it hurts me to have done what I did, I did not harm this man. Not really. I simply took away his special abilities. Please let all the specials know that what I did to this special is the same thing I would do to any felon who uses his special abilities to attempt to kill. We, as specials, cannot allow and will not tolerate specials who are criminal. The fear that this would cause throughout the world would have everyone with a gun shooting at us. It would have children being stoned to death or destroyed. Have the precogs look at what could happen. We, as specials, must maintain an extremely high moral standard. That includes not killing people for the purpose of crime. I am going to ask the president to allow us to punish anyone who gets caught and sentenced. With our telepathy, we won't make mistakes. If someone is guilty of using special abilities to commit a violent crime, then that person doesn't deserve to have those abilities any longer. Self-protection is one thing and expected, but criminals in our ranks will get us all killed and cannot be tolerated. There is no excuse. A bad childhood, forced into it, doing it for country, politics, or making money are not excuses. I cannot order the specials around, and I won't, but I suggest that you put it out to the entire world. We will police our own, and we will not be gentle!"

When I finished there was a deafening round of applause and cheers but not from the specials. The cheers were from all the others. I could see it in the eyes of the specials that they didn't understand.

I said more quietly so that only the specials surrounding me could hear. "A special just tried to kill me. He harmed two guards, and his bullets could have killed others. We were lucky they did not. These great people at this base are our friends, but they are afraid of what we can do. If the people who work with us and protect us are afraid of us, what do you think the rest of the world is like? Having a special kill just one person on the outside would cause a panic that could cause the total annihilation of all specials.

We would be hunted down and destroyed. However, if they see that we are working hard to ensure that they are protected from our kind, they may come to realize that we are their only hope." I turned and left.

I was closely followed by eight of the team, the captain, and the intruder, who was being carried. Once inside home, I touched the intruder's head, and he woke up. I asked, "For whom are you working?"

He tried to use his abilities but looked confused.

"I took away your talents, sir. You can no longer use any of the abilities you had. You're completely normal now."

Tears started to flow from his eyes.

"I'm afraid that what I did is very permanent. No healer can fix the damage I caused. Now I will ask one more time: who are you, and for whom are you working?"

He didn't answer, but he also had no shields.

"I can and will rip it out of your mind if you don't tell me right now."

Susan could see the anger in my face, and she said, "Freddy, that's not necessary."

"I need to know, Susan. I want to know who is trying to kill me and my friends and take my ships. Whoever it is must be removed permanently."

"And what if it's an entire country?"

I looked at her with anger. "Your point?"

"Freddy, I know you're angry. You just lost your project, and now you've been attacked, but you can't harm a person. For goodness' sake, you walk around insects and cry when you see butterflies dead on the windowsill. Think about what you're saying."

I lowered my shoulders with a sigh of resignation. "You're right, of course. But something has to be done. One of my friends could have been hurt!"

"Yes, it does, and yes, we will. I am very sorry that this

happened. However, there will be a full investigation using specials and personnel that have no issues with tearing this man's mind apart. You let me do my job."

"Very well, but I want to see the report you're going to send to the president before you send it. I want to add a note about how quick everyone was to save me and how fast the issue was handled. I don't want her getting the wrong impression and firing you! I will not stand for that. Tell her that a lot of this is about to go away, as we are going to move."

"Move?"

"The war is over, my ships are back, and so I'm moving my home to Mars. Let's see if we have these problems out there." I was suddenly tired. "Susan?"

"Yes, dear."

"I need that vacation."

Sadly, Susan said, "I know."

As I turned to leave, I mumbled, "I wonder if Becky would like to live on Mars."

✦

Gray said, "It has always fascinated me that they fight among themselves so much. It is this practice that has made them strong, but it has also made them weak. They are not a cohesive force." He turned to me and added, "We stopped fighting among ourselves centuries ago. You may be ahead in some things, but you are far behind in others."

I said, "In this, I am ashamed. Even with the knowledge that there are creatures out in space that are waiting to destroy us, there are still those of our own species that would do the same if they could. There is a sickness that goes around in our species. It is called the 'I am right and you are wrong; therefore, I will destroy you so right can prevail' syndrome. The people that have it cannot see correctly and will not try to see the other side. It is a sad thing. It is almost like having an entire population of Grays."

Green and Blue choked, Yellows nearly dropped me, and Black smiled. Black said, "Well, my pen mates will laugh on that one for days. Gray, may I suggest you continue to try to banter with the Red. It is amusing."

A creature the size and color of the Green walked in. He was old and wore a red robe. His arms were folded, and he looked solemn. Green bowed deeply, saying, "Great one, I am honored."

The Red said, "I will watch and learn. Continue, Green."

All the others went very quiet, and Green continued.

✦ ✦ ✦

PREPARATIONS

Commander Daphne Morgan exclaimed, "Moving to Mars! Did I hear Freddy right?"

Susan nodded her head. "It was expected. You know his plans as well as any of us, Commander Morgan, and this is his third step. Step one was build ships. He has completed that issue. Step two was build a city on the moon. We are nearly finished with the building portion of that project. Step three is to colonize Mars, and step four is to colonize the stars. How long did you think we could stall him? If not for his current project, he would have been concentrating on Mars or Oreo or any one of a hundred other planets that are now up for grabs. Now his project is ruined, and his last ship is nearly completed. Notice that no new ship designs have started. The line is closing up, and Freddy has not reprogrammed any robots this month. He is serious about leaving, and after today I am going to do everything I can to help him. No more stalling. We're moving in four to six weeks."

Daphne said, "I wonder what step five is."

Susan smiled and then stood straighter and started barking orders. "Hold assembly, and tell the team everything. I don't want questions. I want readiness, and I want it yesterday."

"I'm on it."

"Thanks, Daphne."

With a snappy salute, Commander Morgan answered, "My pleasure, Captain." She did an about-face and started gathering the team.

Susan continued, "Lieutenant Uniceson! I want to know everything this fool knows," She kicked the prisoner in the face, which knocked him out again and caused him to fall. "Strip his mind. I want everything, and I want it now."

"Yes, ma'am." Lieutenant Uniceson grabbed hold of the man in one hand, lifted him to his feet, and propelled him through the air and into the hands of two waiting marines.

"Chief Peters," Susan said, "I want the president on the hot line, scrambled, in five minutes. If you can tie in Admiral Penn, do so."

"I'm working on it, Captain." He left, heading toward the office.

Susan said, "I'll write a letter to all the parents of the specials and a letter to the specials themselves. We need to inform them—in a very tactful way—that their sons and daughters are not in danger of having Freddy remove their powers. There are going to be rumors about what Freddy did, and I want the truth out there before we start losing key people."

Colleen said, "I'll have a press conference set up for tomorrow. Can you have that letter prepared tonight?"

Susan smiled. "I have already written it. I knew this was going to come up sometime. All I need to do is modify it a little and get approval. I think the president will want a chop."

Colleen laughed. "Always one step ahead, Captain?"

"With Freddy, we need to be much more than one or

two steps ahead. We need to have the game finished before he starts, and I cannot do that as the base commander. That has to change." She tapped her head, thinking. "Freddy has always said that the ships are for moving us to the stars. He has made us promises to save them for that purpose." She smiled. "Let's show him that we keep our promises. I'll ask Admiral Penn to place every available ship at Freddy's disposal. That should help calm him down. If we can keep him interested in building on Mars, we may be able to postpone his star travel. I want the building ships here. We start moving the smaller buildings in about four weeks. The house goes last. I think we can pack the shop's robots and equipment into some of the larger ships. Finish all the current projects, and then start packing. And dismantle that black-hole maker!"

Chief Peters ran out of the office and said, "Captain, Admiral Penn and the president are on line. The media was covering the cake cutting, and now everything is out. The president is most unhappy. There are all kinds of calls. Freddy's little speech was on international television, and there is a general uproar that someone made it onto this base and tried to attack our 'national treasure.' In addition, his attitude toward policing his own went over very big."

"Big?"

"Captain, please let the president explain. This is way over my head."

Susan said, "Very well, Peters. I'll take it in my office." She headed to her office, thinking, *This could be the end of my career or the beginning of a life in space. Either way, I need that vacation as much as Freddy.*

As she entered the office, the president and Admiral Penn stared down at her from a huge split-screen high on the wall. "Good evening, Madam President, Admiral Penn. Hope you're having a better day than I am."

The president was first to respond. "It seems that I was. I'm not fully sure about how my night is going to go."

Admiral Penn was a little cheerier. "Hello, Captain. I hope you have some good news. Our president seems a little put out."

"I don't understand why," Susan said. "Everything is happening exactly as I planned." She heard a giggle in the background.

"She is telling the truth, but she is doing so very loosely, in that she allowed for a lot of flexibility in her planning." Melanie Orgonna was an aide to the president and a niece of Katie Swanson. She was a telepath and empathic and just turned eighteen years old. She could spot a lie, even over the phone.

"Hi, Melanie. Happy birthday."

"Hello, Captain James. How's Freddy?"

"Freddy needs to calm down. He is in his room being watched by your aunt. Madam President, I said that this fell into my plans because Freddy is insisting on going up into space in his new ship. I was looking for a way to stop him, and this attack did the trick."

"How so?"

"As you know, we have been finding all kinds of reasons to stop him or at least postpone the inevitable."

"Yes. The world would be very upset if he died. The jobs he is creating alone have made America stronger than ever before. We just celebrated paying off the national debt. My goodness, he is the best thing this country has had—this world has had—since the invention of the wheel, and people are arguing over that. Most think Freddy is more important. Congress has already stated that they are declaring war on any country, group, or individual that attacks Freddy Anderson. They want a report about this assassin, and they are sending people to get it."

"By the time they get here I'll have every bit of information he has. I have people working on it as we speak. However, this incident and the earlier incident about his latest project have caused a slight postponement in his plans."

Admiral Penn jumped in. "Was Freddy really inventing his own black hole?"

"We stopped him, but a few short seconds more and there would have been a fully functional black hole under where I'm standing."

"My God! I'm glad you stopped him."

"So am I, but he is not very happy about it. He must have worked very hard on the project. Madam President, Freddy wants to be safe. He wants everyone to be safe. He has decided to move to Mars to cut down on possible attacks. I think I can use that to keep him very busy—so busy that going to the stars will be out of the question for a little while. There are some safety issues that just came to my attention, and I think that building a safe place to live up there may take some very creative thinking and time. Lots of time. Meanwhile, Freddy can continue working on projects that will make life easier out in space and on colonies. Mars has eight domes now and plenty of space. There is enough air and shielded protection to keep everyone living there very secure. Freddy can create shops in the mountainsides. He already has a place picked out. He was showing it to me the last time we were there. It's the perfect solution to keeping him in reach and under watch. In addition, I need to spend time with Freddy. I need to cut back to handling things that impact Freddy only. Moving to Mars gives me a perfect excuse to hand over base operations to another."

"After reading your report about his latest project, I was thinking the same thing. Admiral Penn, any suggestions for a base commander?"

"Interesting. I have several, Madam President. I think they will pass the prerequisites."

"Good, call them in, and find out. Captain, you will still have override on anything that affects Freddy. I will not have some base commander crimping Freddy's style. That's your job."

"Thanks. About his little speech to the specials—I hear it's all over the news."

"It is, and don't worry. The entire world is cheering Freddy. Again, he has hit on a problem we didn't even know we had. We have eight specials being prosecuted at this time, for everything from theft to murder. We had no idea what to do with them, but if we use specials to screen them, and if they find them guilty of misuse of their abilities, and if they remove their abilities for doing so with no exceptions, we will be sending two very important messages to the world. First, to us normal people, specials are not special when it comes to breaking the law. Second, to the specials, use your abilities improperly and you will lose them. Did you know that several parents have asked me to have Freddy remove their children's abilities so that they are no longer 'freaks'? We are sending people to help straighten out those parents. If we have to, we will remove the children. We don't need child abuse on top of everything else. They will be watched very closely. The world is sick of people blaming their childhood for all their ills. Frankly, so am I. They like the idea that there are no excuses. Abuse it, and lose it. That's the word going around, and I'm going to back that up fully. Melanie has informed me that people close to me are very happy about this change in policy. They are tired of us catching spies and turning them loose. From now on—and I will inform the rest of the world—if we catch someone, that person will be sent back minus his or her abilities. I think they may keep their people home more. They cannot afford to lose this resource any more than I can,. Tell Freddy that. You tell him I want him on Mars and that we are with him on keeping everyone honest."

"I'll tell him."

Admiral Penn asked, "Need any help moving?"

"Actually, we promised Freddy that his ships would be used for the moves. It was one of the reasons he agreed to make so many."

The president said, "Admiral, while keeping the watch, I would like to see every ship possible helping with this move."

"Consider it done. Captain, tell Freddy that the first ships will be there tonight."

"Wait on that for four weeks, but have shuttles standing by immediately."

"Why wait?"

"We need to plan, and Freddy needs a vacation. I expect that he will want to plan some changes to the Mars site and then start his robots building the space for his shops. After that, we are going away on a working vacation."

"Where?"

"That's classified, Admiral. I will keep in touch, so do not worry. We will take a shuttle with all the gear we need and then disappear for two or three weeks. After that, you may find me asking for an escort to Mars. Then we will be ready to move. Freddy needs to know that his ships are awaiting his needs."

"Believe me, they are."

"That's good, Admiral. Please have two shuttles ready for us to move equipment to start the modifications on Mars. Those two shuttles and the fact you are willing to have most of the fleet here will go a long way toward calming Freddy. Madam President, I will let Freddy know, in a tactful way, that you approve. Normally, he would take it well, as he loves you very much, but right now he might become self-righteous and a little uppity if someone tells him that he needs the approval. After all, he says, 'They are *my* ships, and it's *my* Mars base.'"

They both laughed. The admiral said, "You did say he was upset."

"You don't know the half of it, Admiral. How would you feel if all the plans you've made—all the work you've slaved over for the last six months—just went up in smoke? You busted your head and passed out, and when you came to, you were slapped by a good friend and chewed out in public by a little girl, who then stomped on your toe, and then someone tried to kill you—all in about an hour of real time. That was Freddy's day."

"Good luck, Captain. Sounds like you have a lot on your hands."

"I do, Admiral, and I have a lot to plan out before Freddy gets up in the morning. With Freddy, that could be any time. I have only a few hours to plan out everything."

"Then I suggest you get to it, and stop letting us waste your time."

"Thanks, Madam President. Talk to both of you later."

"Good night, Captain."

Susan sat back, thinking, *Well, that went better than I expected. I wonder who the admiral has in mind for the Mars base. I'll worry about that later. Right now, I have a lot of work. I just hope Freddy is willing to listen. Perhaps—just perhaps—I can talk Becky into visiting Mars when everything is set up.*

✦

The Red said, "So he does have the knowledge to build a black hole. And in that bit there was a shielded suit, teleportation, healing, and healing used as destruction. Why does he not use his destructive healing to attack you?"

Little Yellows stiffened, and so did Green and Big Yellows. They were all touching me.

I said, "That would be rude. Have Gray touch me, though. He reminds me of the army."

Green and the Yellows relaxed a little.

Red said, "So even with two Yellows and a Green trying to block, you can talk through their efforts. I may need to redesign this tank."

I said, "There are many things you could do to make it a better tank." I mentioned a few using physics. He talked back in physics terms. The conversation carried on for several minutes before the Black stopped it.

Black said, "*Red!* You will stop now. We need to know things, and we are running short on time."

Red looked sadly at Black. "I learned more in that short time than I have in the last ten years. I hold you responsible, Black. If you allow this Red to be harmed in any way, there will be war." He crossed his arms and stood quietly. The others could not stop looking at him in amazement. He said, "Well?"

Green continued, after shaking his head to clear his thoughts.

✦ ✦ ✦

RESCUE

I was having a nightmare about some dark force harming Becky. I must have been screaming, as Colleen came in, as well as Marian.

Colleen shook me. "Freddy, wake up! Freddy! Wake *up*!"

Marian took my hand and bent my finger back.

With the pain, I groggily became aware of my surroundings. "*Ouch*! What's going on?"

Colleen said, "You were having a nightmare. You were yelling out 'Save Becky' at the top of your lungs."

Everything came rushing back to me, and I quickly got up and started dressing.

Colleen asked, "What are you doing? It was only a nightmare."

"No, Colleen. Becky's in trouble. I can feel it."

Colleen started helping me dress. "Are you sure, Freddy?"

"Yes."

Marian contacted the watch. "Denise, Freddy says Becky is in trouble. Contact the town watch, find out anything you can, and ensure they are on high alert."

The watch answered, "I'm on it, Marian. Several specials are on the way. Freddy must have woken them."

"Understood."

Marian said, "Freddy, the watch is checking on Becky at the Seaward Inn. She is probably all right."

I looked up just long enough to say, "Marian, Becky is not at the inn. She has been kidnapped. I'm going after her. You with me, or do I go alone?"

Colleen said, "Home."

"Yes."

"Scan for Becky Crain at the Seaward Inn, and report."

"*Working. Becky Crain is not at the Seaward Inn.*"

"Check the town."

"*Working. Becky Crain is not in town.*"

Shop broke in. "*Colleen, I have run a check, and Becky is not detectable on the planet.*"

Marian's hand flew to her mouth, "Oh, my God!"

I said, "Shop! Have K1 power up."

"*Very well, Freddy. Your new ship is coming on line.*"

"When she is at full power, use the transporter and teleport her outside."

"*She is at full power, and I will be able to teleport her in three minutes. She wants orders.*"

"Tell her that I want her to go to stationary orbit and look for Becky through all modes. I sense Becky is in the air somewhere over the Atlantic Ocean."

"*She understands, Freddy, and will do so and report.*"

Marian took hold of me so that I would not fall over, trying to get my foot into the wrong shoe. Colleen came around and saw the problem, saying, "The other foot, Freddy. That's the left shoe."

Two of my special friends came running into the room at about the same time as the Captain.

Captain Susan James said in a commanding tone, "Stop!"

No one in the room moved an inch, and for some silly reason, every one of us look guilty.

"What in the blazes is going on in here?"

I seldom see Susan in this mood, but when she is, it's scary. Both my special friends started to back out, and Susan said in a quiet voice that would have made a speeding train stop, "Don't you even think about moving." Susan surveyed the room. "Colleen, why does everyone in this room look guilty?"

Colleen said, "I'll explain that later, Captain. Right now, we have an emergency."

"Report."

"I believe Becky Crain has been kidnapped and is in a plane over the Atlantic as we speak."

The captain yelled, "Shop!"

"I have scanned the traffic over the Atlantic, Captain, and none of the 264 planes has Becky aboard."

I had my left shoe on my right foot now and was working on the right shoe when K1 said, *"Freddy, I have finished the scans of all planes over the Atlantic Ocean. One plane has a box inside with a magnetic field surrounding it. I have penetrated the field, and Becky is in the box. She is drugged, tied up, crying, and afraid. She is gagged, but she is calling your name."*

I stopped what I was doing and put one hand on each of my friends' arms.

Rodney Brown was eighteen years old and a strong telekinetic, easily capable of lifting a medium-sized ship, though not for long. He looked like he could lift them without the kinetics, as he was a big, heavily muscled, high-school football star. However, he was not very intelligent. He was very street-wise, but he could not obtain a high enough score to get into college, even on a football scholarship. Rodney was in prison for lifting a train and setting it back down—and none too gently. During a meeting with several specials who worked in a charity group, they found out that the train was about to hit a busload of primary-school children. He quickly became a hero but was placed into our custody just the same. The official's words were, "Just in case." Rodney was drawn to beauty and intelligence and that led him to pair up with Georgia.

Seventeen-year-old Maxine Stump, aka Georgia Peach, was a great telepath with the added ability of placing thoughts inside a mind with pictures. The person receiving the thought would know it wasn't his, but he would receive it. She won several beauty pageants but missed out on the Miss Teen America by a small margin, and she didn't even cheat. She was highly intelligent but not street-wise at all. Rodney was in love with her. It was her Southern accent that caught him. She came from a family that did not like her abilities. They tried to kill her in her sleep, and nearly everyone with any telepathy heard her cry for help. Maxine loved big, strong men who could protect her from people like her family. She also liked men without too much intelligence. That way, she could control them. Rodney was the perfect sucker. They were inseparable.

I said to them, "Please let me borrow your energy." Both nodded, and I reached inside them, and we became as one. We reached out, found the ship and found the box, and I penetrated the outer magnetic shielding, the three feet of steel-reinforced concrete, eight different types of metal linings, some strange type of liquid, and a plastic liner—and there was my Becky.

I touched her mind gently and said, "Hello, my love."

"Freddy?"

"Yes, sweetheart."

"Freddy! Oh, Freddy. Help me! Please help me!"

"Of course I am going to help you. Would I let the girl I love so very much fall into the hands of fools?"

A tiny bit of my Becky's feisty spirit shone through for just a second. "You just did!"

I smiled and let her feel my love and amusement. Then I filled her with calm and reassurance. "I will be there shortly. I cannot hold this contact for long. Wait for me, my darling."

The last thing I heard was, "Where am I going to go, you idiot? Oh, Freddy, I didn't mean it that way. Freddy? Freddy!"

I let go of Rodney and Georgia, and our union collapsed. Georgia playfully hit Rodney on the arm. "Why don't you love me like that?"

Rodney answered, "If I were tied up, gagged, and stuffed in a dark box, and you were my only hope of rescue, I would love you any way you wanted."

She looked up at him with evil eyes and said, "That can be arranged."

I paid little attention to them as I was working out a plan to save my Becky.

The captain saw this and said, "Freddy, think out loud so we know what you're planning. Colleen, get the team ready. Freddy, how is Becky? I assume that was what you were doing—contacting Becky."

Colleen said, "Half are already in body armor and waiting, Captain. The other half will be ready in seconds."

I said in a tone that revealed both immense worry and great joy, "Becky loves me again." Then I said angrily, "How many ships do we have at the base at this time, Captain James?"

Susan knew I was livid. She knew from my tone and the fact that I called her Captain James. She answered, "Eight ships arrived during the night to help with the move. Three are destroyer escort class. The rest are shuttles and one building mover."

I was a little shocked, as I thought I'd have to argue

to obtain help from my ships. "Susan, I'm not ready to move yet."

"I know, and I told them to wait for four weeks. They want to help so badly that they came anyway."

"Good. I want a destroyer escort ready to go now. We are going to pull that box out of that plane, and I will open it myself."

"How is Becky doing?" Susan repeated.

Now that I had made contact I could at least hold my tag on her. And with that tag, I could feel her emotions. "Susan, she is horribly frightened, but now that she knows we know and that we are coming to rescue her, she has become her spirited self."

Susan saw my worry. "Good. Freddy, does Becky know that box has a deadly trap?"

"No." I looked up at Susan, thinking, *I can never get anything past her.* Out loud, I said, "And she never will."

Henry came in. "Captain, the troops are ready, and all three destroyer escorts are standing by."

I looked out my window and teleported every one of them onto the quarterdeck of the first destroyer escort I saw. "Captain, we're ready to go."

As shocked as the Captain of the *Harm's Way* was to have thirty armed SEALs and eight specials on his quarterdeck, he quickly adjusted and started giving orders. We took off, and within three minutes we were directly over the plane, five miles up.

Rodney turned to the specials and asked, "How did you get here?"

Joe Crysem was a twenty-four-year old major empath. He had the ability to make people feel any way he wanted, and he knew exactly how people felt around him. It made him great at crowd control. Joe answered, "You think you're the only one who cares about Becky? Besides, two clairvoyants said we would be needed."

I looked over and said, "And I sent for them mentally." I turned to Susan, saying, "I need to send SEALs into that plane to knock out everyone. There are twenty-six people. Someone will have to quickly take over flying. Please prepare." I turned to the specials and said, "Joe, please use your empathy and spread confidence and peace throughout that ship. I need them thinking they got away with this. Mally, I am glad to see you here. Can you sense the plane below us?"

Mally looked up at me with big eyes and said, "Yes, big brother." She gave me a hug.

Mally was eight years old, and I looked at her as a little sister. She'd had a bad childhood, and I tried to make it up to her with as much loving kindness as possible, without spoiling her—well, not too much spoiling. She had the ability to scan anything, sense through almost anything, and stop movement on a molecular level. I stroked her hair lovingly. "Now look closer. See the man with his finger tied to a switch."

"I see him. He's a bad man. He has bad thoughts."

"Yes, he is. Can you make it so that the switch will not move?"

She smiled. "Yes. I can do that."

"Mally, this is very important. If he moves that switch, your big sister Becky will die."

Mally started tearing up and said, "He's not going to move that switch. No one will ever move that switch!"

"Thank you, princess." I turned to Susan. "Once everything is secured, I will come onboard to remove Becky."

"Understood. We're ready."

"Good. Here you go."

I teleported twenty-nine SEALs into the ship in various areas and one directly into the cockpit. The battle was quick and deadly. One kidnapper tried to turn the switch. He only had that one try before he died. Susan took no chances with him having a second switch. Three SEALs were stationed at that console. Katie sent a mental signal: *"All secure, Freddy."*

As soon as everything was done, I teleported down and mentally scanned the equipment. Susan was right next to me. "It's trapped in several ways, Susan," I said, "and there is a magnetic field with a strange, fluctuating electrical frequency around this box, caused by some of the equipment on this plane, that stops me from teleporting her out without having my hands directly on the box." Then I reached out and teleported Johnny Cannon down. Johnny looked confused, so I gave him a second to adjust to suddenly being someplace else. Johnny was fifteen going on forty. He had the ability to change toxics into pure water. No one has figured out how, but he will have a great and everlasting high-paying job when he graduates from our school.

"Johnny."

Johnny heard me and came my direction. "I wish you wouldn't teleport me without giving me warning. Darn, that's irritating."

"Sorry. I'm in a hurry. Touch my arm." Once he did, I said, "What I'm showing you is Becky inside the box."

"I see her. Nice teddy."

"Johnny!"

"Okay. Don't get jealous."

I stopped myself growling and concentrated on saving my Becky. "Do you see that liquid surrounding her in that plastic layer?"

"Yes. Nasty stuff."

"What is it?"

"Some sort of highly oxygenated acid. Much stronger than sulfuric."

"Can you change it?"

"Sure."

I felt his energy flow through me and into the box. It took several minutes, but slowly, after what seemed like years, the liquid was water. Johnny collapsed next to me. I teleported him to the quarterdeck of the *Harm's Way* and sent a mental to Trisha to take care of him.

Trisha Zoemal was thirteen but thought she was eighteen—and acted like she was twelve. She was the third best healer known, and she had the added ability to help burned-out specials. I did not intend to burn out anyone, though, and Johnny was far from it.

Trisha instantly checked him and reported he was still weak but would be fine.

Susan said, "I don't see a lid or opening."

I answered, "There isn't one. She was teleported inside before the magnetic field was turned on." I got up and checked everyone on the ship. There were only twenty-five. We scanned and tore the ship apart. The *Harm's Way* was warned, and they scanned and triple-checked everyone and every place. The monster was not found. Somehow, he'd escaped. I say "monster" because only a monster would dream up a cage like this. If the switch had been turned or the magnetic field dropped before a certain unknown time, Becky would have been submerged in acid that would keep her alive and awake until most of her body was painfully eaten away. Thanks to Johnny, now she would only drown. "What to do ... what to do." Then it hit me, and I teleported Lisa and Chuck down into the plane. As I expected, they were kissing.

Chuck "the Octopus" Stewart was sixteen years old—a

sports-minded high-school quarterback and basketball star. Nicknamed Octopus for reasons I won't discuss, he had the ability to temporarily weaken metal to the breaking point or strengthen it to beyond anything known. He loved Lisa Ann because she was a cheerleader and easy, though being easy had nothing to do with cheerleading.

Lisa Ann was fifteen, head cheerleader, and a sports nut. She was born and raised on a pig farm, and she developed an uncanny ability to import fresh air and breathe for everyone around her. She would be of great use in ambulances to give air to people who were not breathing. She loved Chuck because of his sports ability—and "a great kisser."

"Stop that, you two." I said.

Lisa Ann said, "Jealous."

Chuck said, "Be serious, Lisa Ann. The team needs us. Sorry, Freddy." Then he kissed Lisa Ann again and let her go. "What do ya need?"

"Chuck, I need both of you to touch me so we can focus together."

They both came over and touched me.

Chuck said, "Lisa! Not there!" Then he took her hand off my chest and moved it to my arm, tsking at Lisa. She pouted but kept her hand on my arm. I showed them Becky, and Lisa became very serious.

"Lisa, when I break the connection to the magnetic shield, the bag of water surrounding Becky will break. She needs you to breathe for her."

"No problem, Freddy."

"Chuck, notice the metal shackles on her ankles and arms as well as around her waist and neck?"

"I see 'em."

"I can't break them; they are too strong and are magnetically shielded."

"Just a sec." Chuck concentrated for a few seconds and said, "You can break them now."

"Thanks. Ready, Lisa?"

"Ready."

I tripped the connection that removed the shielding. Water started pouring in, and Becky started to panic. I telekinetically pulled gently on all six shackles, and they snapped, cutting off the magnetic shielding. Then I teleported her into my arms. With tears, I held her to me. Susan brought a blanket and laid it on her.

Becky leaned into me and sobbed with relief.

After a short while, I pulled down her gag and kissed her. She kissed back willingly and with great happiness.

Becky pulled back and said, "You can untie me now."

I looked at her and said, "I don't know. This seems the only way I can sneak a kiss without getting slapped. I kind of like you this way."

"Freddy!"

"Okay, okay." I undid her bonds, and she threw her arms around me and kissed me again. I teleported everyone except six SEAL team members back aboard the *Harm's Way*, and we headed home. The six SEALs turned the plane around and headed back with the evidence. At the Seaward Inn, Miss Crain, Johnny, Annabel, and Carroll were waiting with open arms. We all received hugs and thank-yous before returning to the base. The next day the fishing ship *Daddy's Dream* made a visit.

✦

Black ordered, "Body Proper, they have and use the ability to teleport aboard ships! Search and protect!" Then he did something mental, and shortly afterward eight

Blacks marched into the room. "The enemy has the ability to teleport into our ship and ranks. The creature in this tank is to be protected. I do not care if the others are destroyed. You will ensure that this one is kept here and unmolested."

This new Black said, "Understood." He looked over at the Gray leader and said, "We do not need these Grays. They are in our way."

The Gray leader made a motion with his hand, and the other Grays eagerly left.

The new Black glared at the others but bowed to the Red, and that bow was deep. The Red paid him no attention, as if the Black was far below him.

The Red said, as if making a list, "Scanners that see through any metal, ships that take off and move through atmosphere at near light-speed, this 'Shop' that can scan the entire world and find a single person, people that teleport, ships that teleport, healing, changing molecular structure with their minds, clairvoyance, telepathy, telekinesis, empathy, and teddy." He paused and then asked, "What is a teddy?"

Green said, "I do not know, sire. I would expect it is something we have never heard about."

Yellows said, "The Body Proper said that we once had a little girl who had a 'teddy' with her. It was a toy, but she held on to it as if it were the most precious thing in the world. They believe it is some kind of creature that children keep as pets."

Red said, "That does not sound correct. Little Yellows, I see you are smiling. Do you know something?"

Little Yellows said, "He just showed us with a picture in his mind what a teddy is. True, a stuffed toy animal is also called a teddy, but in this case, it is a type of nightclothes. A very sexy type of nightclothes."

Red said, "We have spent many years coming down

to this planet and borrowing their people, and we know nothing about them. Perhaps the Red that I placed in charge of the expedition was not a good fit. I would look into it, but he is on the mother ship, along with eighteen other Reds. Green, please continue."

CHAPTER 23

✦ ✦ ✦

RELUCTANCE

I was working in my room. Sadly, Susan will not allow me in the shop until after we "have a talk." Word came up that the Crain family was pulling in on their fishing boat, the *Daddy's Dream*. I ran down the stairs and headed out to the docks. Susan caught me at the bottom of the stairs and accompanied me, along with five of the team.

The *Daddy's Dream* was just rounding the last corner, headed into the main waters of home base, when I reached the pier. The boat was flanked and dwarfed by two of our shuttles, which were scanning and ensuring that only approved personnel were aboard. They were still too far away to make out much detail.

"I wonder why the visit," Susan said. "For goodness' sake, we just saw them last night. Something's up. I can feel it."

I looked over at her and teasingly said, "I think you're developing some talent."

She looked at me with a grin. "I don't need talent to know that Captain Crain does not put off fishing at this time of year for anything short of funerals and weddings for close relatives. And then it depends on how close the relative is."

I mentally reached out toward the boat and felt the emotions. "He's sad."

"What?"

I looked up at Susan and repeated, "He's sad. They're all sad."

Georgia Peach walked up and said, "They have to do something they do not want to do, and it's because of you, Freddy. Captain Crain does not blame you fully but does see you as the reason he has to do this and holds you responsible."

The boat was getting close enough that I could just make out Becky, Johnny, and Carroll standing in the forward section, waving. The waving was not enthusiastic.

I turned to Georgia Peach and asked, "What does he hold me responsible for?"

"Becky. That's all I can see. It's not polite to look closer."

Rodney gave Georgia a comforting hug and added, "I don't need telepathy to see what's going on."

"What?" I asked.

"Last night Becky was kidnapped. The entire family was placed in danger, and she wasn't kidnapped because of you. She was taken because she is a special, slightly talented in empathy. For goodness' sake, Freddy, stop working long enough to smell the roses or at least watch the news. There has been a rash of child kidnappings lately."

"There has?"

Susan said, "Yes, there has. The president is working on the issue, and we believe the culprits died in that plane last night, but the kingpin is still out there. He is well funded and capable of doing anything. Why he wants the specials, we don't know, but he is willing to go to long lengths to capture as many as he can get his hands on. It's why you were attacked. They consider you the only one capable of stopping them."

Chuck Stewart added, "Why do you think we have so many specials showing up at this base? Every special is being shipped here or to the ranch."

Susan said, "Actually, they're all being sent here. They're going to be dispersed into the fleet and Luna City, and many will be coming to Mars with us, and that includes some of the families. The specials need protection until they are old enough to protect themselves."

"How many specials?"

"Five hundred for the fleet, one hundred for Luna City, and 280 will be going to Mars. Counting family, Mars will have a group of about eight hundred."

"Eight hundred!"

Susan smiled and said, "Now don't get upset, Freddy. Almost all of the ones we are taking are farmers. We have a need for them anyway. By the time we return home from vacation, all will be on Mars in the main dome.

I looked somewhat skeptically at Susan. "You going to try to run Mars with all those specials aboard?"

She smiled at me. "No. We have someone else in mind for commander of Mars, and he is a special."

I was shocked and full of a thousand questions. Where would they all live? What about food and water? How could we handle all the safety problems? However, the *Daddy's Dream* was now pulling up to the dock, and Becky was looking at me in a strange way. As soon as the boat moored and the plank let down, the captain walked off, looking red-eyed and very upset. For some reason everyone else stayed aboard. I saw Susan's stance change just the tiniest bit, and I quickly stepped between the two captains. I put out my hand. "Hello, Captain Crain. To what do I owe this visit?" I looked past him and waved to Becky, but she did not wave back.

"Freddy, again I will thank you for saving my Becky." He did not take my hand.

"You're welcome, sir."

"I hear that all specials are transferring out for their own protection. Is this correct?"

I gave a quick look at Susan and then addressed Captain Crain. "I was just informed of that myself."

"Freddy, Becky explained to us this morning that she wasn't kidnapped because of you, though I find that hard to believe. She explained that she heard her kidnappers say that they need several more for some experiment."

"Did she tell this to the FBI?"

"Yes. Everyone knows that you take in specials like my Becky and that you're going away to Mars with them. Is that true?"

"Yes."

Captain Crain turned around and motioned to Becky, and then he turned back to me. "I will not have my Becky in constant danger."

Becky was helped down the plank, and two of the boat's crew brought her baggage. As soon as she was down, Captain Crain gave her one last hug. With sadness in his voice, he said to me, "I hold you fully responsible for my daughter's welfare, Freddy." He turned away and ordered, "Plank in. Lines away," as he boarded the *Daddy's Dream*.

Becky watched as he pulled out. She turned to me and kissed me on the cheek, and then she slapped me hard and asked, "Who is Julia?"

✦

Green said, "That's interesting. Why slap him if she loves him?"

Red said, "A long time ago, before the time of the Mad Change, there was a time when our people were not telepathic. Females would torment the males something horrible when they wanted attention. If another female tried to steal that attention, there would be a fight. After the fight, to bring the attention back into focus for the males, the females would beat them until they passed out. I think this slapping is a mild form of the same type of ritual. Notice she mentioned another female."

Green said, "But they are telepathic. This would not work."

Red said, "He is. Is she? They are new at being telepathic. They have not developed the culture for it. They are just starting the Mad Change."

Everyone looked at me as if I had the black plague. The Black said, "That fits. They are kidnapping the ones with special abilities for experiments. Did we not do the same?"

Red answered, "Yes, and that started the Great War. Our Blues did nothing and our—what did he call them? 'Specials?'—our specials fought back. The specials killed all of the others. It was a long, dark time in our history."

Green said, "Their Blues are fighting for them. They want the specials. They are protecting them."

Blue said, "Perhaps their Blues are smarter than ours were."

The others looked downcast. Green said, "Perhaps I should continue."

I said, "Good idea."

They all looked at me as if to yell, "Quiet!"

CHAPTER 24

✦ ✦ ✦

BETS

"**B**ecky! What was that slap for?"

Becky pulled a newspaper clipping from her pocket and handed it to me. "So you're taking some girl on vacation with you? Just you and her, alone in the woods for two months. Then you're going to take her to Mars with you. How *could* you?"

At first I was shocked, but one of the problems with being empathic is that I can tell when someone is trying to pull something. Becky did not really believe the newspaper. She wanted to set controls, right from the start. I had been around the team and a lot of females for too long to fall for that, and I wasn't about to allow my life to be run by another female—not even if I truly loved her.

I turned to Susan and said, "If Becky is going to be foolish enough to believe what she reads in the newspaper, then fine." I turned toward home, pretending to be in a temper, and started walking. I sent a telepathic message to all the empaths and telepaths who were watching. Leaving Becky out, I said, *"Don't let on."* I tried to sound disappointed when I said, "I'm going to my room to work on what needs to happen on Mars. Please have Miss Crain housed in the dormitory with the other specials. See to her needs but nothing special."

Becky watched in shock as I left. She did not know I would watch telepathically so I could see the outcome.

Susan smiled as she turned to Becky and said, "I know what you just tried to pull. Every woman here has tried that kind of stuff or used their feminine wiles on Freddy at one point or another. It doesn't work. He sees right through it. You keep trying that kind of foolishness on the strongest special known, and your life is going to be full of heartache, child."

Georgia Peach took Becky by the arm and started walking with her to the dorm. "You've been pulling that crap on boys that are not special and it works real well," she told Becky. "Believe me when I say that I know. But now you're with people who can instantly see exactly what you're trying to do. Follow my lead, and I'll teach you how to own Freddy, and he won't even know what happened."

Becky was in tears as she turned and said, "My luggage."

Georgia said, "Don't worry, Becky." Then she turned to Rodney and said, "Rodney will bring Becky's luggage. Won't you, dear?"

Rodney smiled big, saying, "Sure, baby doll."

Becky watched and nearly tripped as her luggage lifted off the ground and started following them.

Georgia reached up and kissed Rodney on the cheek fondly, saying, "Showoff."

Susan smiled, thinking, *Oh yes. Freddy is going to be way too busy to go into space.*

The specials watched Freddy leave the area while telepathically laying bets.

Johnny said, *"Two dollars says he doesn't make it."*

Trisha said, *"You're on."*

Chuck added, *"I'll take that bet also."*

Johnny said, *"Got ya. Anyone else want in on this?"* No one else bet, but they were all watching.

Freddy entered the house before he nearly busted a gut with laughing so hard.

"All right, pay up, Johnny."

"Darn. I was sure he couldn't hold it that long. All right, here." He took four dollars from his wallet and passed it out.

Joe Crysem said, "I think most of his happiness was relief that Becky is now well protected and safe."

Susan followed me into the house and waited for me to calm down before nonchalantly saying, "Georgia Peach just took Becky away to teach her how to handle men that are specials." That put a quick stop to my laughter.

"Susan, that's not a good thing. She and Lisa Ann will gang up on Becky and teach her all kinds of bad habits. I won't stand a chance!"

"You set it up so she's in the dorms with them."

"Maybe we should bring her into the house."

"No. She's not properly trained yet. She stays in the dorms for now."

"But Susan—"

"No! Perhaps if you are good between now and the move to Mars, I may allow her to live in the same Mars dome."

Skeptically, I asked, "Any chance you'll house the other two in a different dome?"

"Not likely."

"That's what I thought." I left for my room, with plans of becoming a hermit running through my head.

✦

Little Yellows laughed, "He is funny. If his entire race is like this, we should keep them around for the entertainment."

Big Yellows said, "We would like that also. No wonder Green and Red have spent so many years watching them."

Red said, "I have seen the reports, and they have people just for making you laugh. They are called comedians. Better than that, they have something called rednecks. I am told that they are the funniest of all the comedians. We concentrated on capturing rednecks just for the laugh. Being comedians, they are born and raised to tell tall tales. It is so funny. When we let them lose, no one believed them. They were perfect for research. We would sometimes make designs in their fields, just to mess with them. They showed everyone, and no one believed a thing they said. It was hilarious."

Gray said, "It's not hilarious now. Many have died, and now we find he has another ship. What is a K1?"

Black said, "Gray is correct. This is not funny. Green, continue, and let's hope we find out about more technology."

C H A P T E R   2 5

✦ ✦ ✦

MURDER

had other plans I needed to make. With Becky along, I
needed to ensure that Mars would be very safe. I set up
a decoy, and then I used the transmitter in my bedroom to
teleport to my retreat, and I started working on plans for
Mars housing, shops, and farming. We were going to need
a lot of food, and growing it ourselves would be best. No
toxins and no hormone additives in the food I will grow
or the cows that eat it. It was two days later that Susan
called me down for dinner. Home informed Shop, and I
teleported to my bedroom and cleaned up. Colleen came
up and ensured that I wore the proper attire. Apparently,
we had guests.

"Who's here, Colleen?"

"It's summer break, so Julia and her mother, Aggie, are
here. So is Congressman Styles and Senator McConner. And,
just for your information, the moment you teleported into
your special area, Susan contacted Shop and found out what
you were doing. The specials saw right through the decoy."

"I'll have to work on that." Changing the subject quickly
before I received a lecture, I asked, "Congressman Styles?
Didn't he run against President Kabe four years ago?"

"Yes, and he almost won."

I pulled on one of my best jumpers. "What's he doing here?"

"It's an election year, and President Kabe cannot run again. She's already had two terms."

"Oh, darn. What's he want?"

"He probably wants your support. Not having it last time lost him the election."

"Have any of the specials checked him out?"

"They can't, and they were not too happy about it. He wears a helmet that clouds his thoughts. He says that he is on the armed services committee and has top-secret information he has to protect. You need to be polite. He is a powerful person."

"We'll see. You know I don't like politics."

"Then be good for the rest of us. He may end up being our boss, and it appears that the House and Senate may become aligned with him."

"So we may change from a Democratic president and House with a Republican Senate to a fully Republican-run federal government?"

"That is possible."

"Oh well. I really don't care. Just as long as he leaves me and mine alone."

Colleen looked at me rather sternly, saying, "You're only two and a half years away from being of legal age to vote. You need to start paying attention, young man."

"Yes, Colleen." I knew when she used that tone of voice that it was useless to argue.

We headed downstairs and into the dining room. The table was already set, and most people were already seated. I was introduced to several people, and we shook hands. I said hello to Julia and her mother, and then turned my attention to a man with a wonderful smile and a pleasant yet intimidating presence.

Susan did the introductions. "Freddy, this is Congressman Styles."

He seemed a natural leader with a lot of charisma. I could see why people liked him so much. The helmet was more a skull cap that was attached to his head via several straps running around his head. I could feel the magnetic signature, and it matched the box Becky had been in. The hair raised on the back of my neck, and I went into defensive mode. Susan saw, and her stance changed. Smiling, I put my hand out, saying, "It's nice to finally meet you in person, sir."

He looked at my hand, hesitating only slightly, and then shook it as quickly and politely as possible and tried to let go. No good; I had tactile contact and easily bypassed his electrical shield. What I saw had nothing to do with being on the armed services committee or top-secret information. I jerked my hand away and ducked behind Susan. The team was on him in a second.

Susan ordered him held and then turned to me. "Freddy, please tell me why I just arrested Congressman Styles in front of the media and on national television?"

I looked up at her and said, "Because that's not Congressman Styles."

Susan looked intently at me. "How do you know, Freddy?"

"With tactile contact, his electrical shield is useless when you're as strong as I am. The real Congressman Styles has five children, correct?"

"Yes."

"Then why is this one thinking how much he hates kids and is glad he doesn't have any? In addition, he thinks specials should be destroyed. That shielding he is wearing has an exact fluctuating signature as the shield on the box that Becky was in. Same electrical frequency and same technology. This is one of the kidnappers."

Susan's face did not change, her body made no sign of a change, but her mind and voice were ice. I shivered. She ordered, "Remove that shield." He tried to stop them, stating that the national secrets he held could not be revealed and that I had no right to do this. His head snapped back, and blood started dripping from his mouth and nose. Susan hit him so hard and so fast I did not see it until after the fact. In a calm voice, she said, "Hold still."

The shield was removed, and I immediately knew what was wrong. "Susan, our good Congressman Styles has been murdered, and this man took his place. They used one of my AutoDoctors to map Congressman Styles's features, eyes, voice, and fingerprints and changed this man's features to match. They did this before using a special to strip the congressman's mind, which slowly killed him. They used that information to train this man to mimic the congressman. My question is, what AD did you use and where?"

He did not say a word, but he did not have to. I said, "Susan, it was on the ES *Protectress*. Someone named Ensign Corvine let them in and showed them how to use it. Please contact the captain and have him use specials to check his crew. And take this fool out of my home."

The team took the kidnapper—or whatever he was— away, and Susan started giving orders. I knew the man was about to go through the worst time of his life, with military and specials that did not have the issues I have with harming anyone. I nearly felt sorry for him for a second. Then I thought of Becky and what they tried to do, and the sympathy went away. The team went outside, arrested the spy's entire group, and confiscated the helicopter. The *Protectress* was given the information, but they did not need it, as they were watching when the spy was taken. Our team checked everything around home and the helicopter to ensure no bombs were aboard and then reported back. Meanwhile, I did a quick check on Senator McConner. No problem there.

The media were frantically talking into their microphones. Julia looked up at her mother and said, "See? I told you. Anything and everything can happen around Freddy. It's never boring. Of course, it would be nicer if Freddy did not have Becky hanging on him." She looked directly at me with that knowing smile, just waiting for me to say something for her magazine. She added, "You know, Becky was giving me the evil eye when I showed up." I turned red, and her smile increased. It was going to be a long two weeks in the woods with Julia.

Dinner resumed, and I had the chance to talk to the other personnel that arrived. Most people were very quiet and sad. Some left to grieve and contact the family of the late congressman. Phone calls were made to try to mitigate the knowledge the kidnapper had gained while on the armed services committee. I tried to lighten things up a little with conversation. Senator David McConner was now the center of attention. He actually had tears over the loss of his old friend. He was running under Styles's ticket for the position of vice president, and the media asked many questions but kept looking at me to see if the answers were true. Earth Force Senator McConner was a staunch Irish Republican, and he answered all our questions easily and candidly, if somewhat solemnly. He was a good man with children and grandchildren that he loved dearly. One of his grandchildren was a special, and he personally ensured her safety and well-being. Apparently, she worked for the government, screening candidates for high positions in the space fleet.

I told him, "David, you should run for our highest office. You're a good man, honest, and a highly capable leader. You would ensure that all children, special or not, are taken care of, and that means no war unless absolutely necessary."

"Thank you, Freddy. I will miss Congressman Styles. He was a good friend. Now I know why he had become so distant lately."

The dinner went well, although it was a little quiet. After the initial issue, Julia asked a few questions.

"Freddy, I'm told that you want to write a column for the magazine. Is that true?"

"Yes, it is."

"That's very nice of you." She looked skeptical and asked, "Why?"

"I have a few ideas about math that I would like to see published. I plan on making a mathematical puzzle that builds on ideas. How often will the magazine be published?"

"We're hoping for once a month."

"Good, then in one year, I can have twelve mathematical ideas out to the public. Each one will build off the last idea. At the end of one year I will grant ten winners of the final puzzle a trip to Mars—if they pass the screening requirements. That would include you and your legal guardian, as you will need to be in charge of them. Susan will work out the details with you about the trip to Mars, but I will write the puzzle." I looked over at Susan, and she nodded.

Julia said, "That's great!"

I smiled. "The following year I may be able to grant ten lucky winners a trip to Oreo or maybe Ganza."

Julia nearly fainted, and her mother put her arm around her. Julia looked up into her mother's eyes, and it was easy to see that I had just granted Julia every wish she'd ever had. Julia looked at me, and her face turned almost gleeful. "I don't suppose Becky will be coming along. Will she?"

"I'll probably bring her, just to keep you in line."

Anger crossed Julia's face for only a second, and I resolved right then and there to ensure that Becky and Julia never met. That would be explosive. I will never understand women!

Susan stood up and said, "We have a long day ahead of us tomorrow, preparing for the trip. I want to thank Senator McConner for his visit and apologize once more for the earlier issue. I can see by the amount of food that wasn't eaten that the death of Congressman Styles has hit us all very hard, and we will need time to grieve. Aggie and Julia, if you'll go with Colleen, she will show you to your rooms."

✦

Blue said, "They killed a Blue to put their own in office. I have never heard of something so sick."

Green said, "It was not this group that did it. They found out and stopped it."

I said, "When working with humans, always remember that most of us are good people, but there are some who will do anything to get their own way. Be careful, but do not blame the entire species due to the acts of a few."

Black looked at Blue and Gray and said, "When working with us, most of us are great, but some are trying to be greater, and their push to reach the top makes them dangerous. Be careful, but do not judge us all on the acts of a few."

Big Yellows said, "We cannot believe the similarities between our two species. It is amazing."

Gray said, "Yes, too bad they have to die."

Green said, "Maybe not. We may be able to save a few and use them."

They all laughed except Little Yellows. She said, "He is not worried."

Red said, "He should not be. He will be one of the ones saved."

I didn't say anymore. I had messed with the new connections to this tank, and I did not want them changing anything, especially as I had to fool with the meter each time the Green brought it in and before he left. I was getting stronger.

C H A P T E R 2 6

✦ ✦ ✦

VACATION

There wasn't really much for me to do in planning for the vacation. The equipment was packed, and I showed the boxes to Susan so she could have them stored away for the trip. First thing in the morning, we loaded up and took off. Julia and her mom, Susan and I, and twenty of the team headed out for some place only Susan knew of—or so I thought.

I monitored the science station, and as we approached the island, I noticed that eight of my ships were stationed where they could not be seen. Three were surrounding the island under water, and five were in the space station, keeping directly above. I turned to Susan, asking, "Do you realize that with eight ships watching us, the entire world knows where we are?"

"Yes, I do, and don't worry about it. Two of those ships are blocking satellites that could watch us, and the rest are for protection. They have orders that no one monitors or reaches this island for the next two weeks except them. If any planes or ships even begin to head this way, they will be warned to head back immediately or face consequences they will not want. I could not find a place where we could hide, now that your scanners are used by the entire world. However, I could make this uninhabited island ours and safe for the next two weeks."

Colleen and the other team members were reading the operation manuals for the items I brought. She looked up and said, "I hope no one can see us. Freddy, can these actually allow us to fly?"

"Of course. Best way I could think up to negotiate rough terrain on a new planet. Still, flying takes up a lot of energy, and you will need to rest often."

Susan asked, "We use our own energy to fly?"

I held up one of the belts. "The belt is adjustable to any size waist. Because it's army green, it looks like a standard utility belt with a small, thin, sealed box, painted camouflage, attached to the back where it is out of the way. There are several clips for attaching other items." I had installed on each a canteen three small pouches and a good army utility knife. I said, "You use your own energy for everything that has to do with these belts. I call them vampirism survival belts. I can put energy packs in them, if needed, but I wanted to try out something different and see if people like it."

Patricia looked over at me and asked, "If I work too hard in this belt, will I run completely out of energy and die?"

"No." I looked at her, smiling. "Would you do that now? Of course not. You would become tired and need to rest. The belt is like an extension of yourself. You put it on, and it taps into your body energy. If you wish to walk, the belt stores all wasted energy. The body radiates energy, and much of that radiation is wasted. The belt harnesses that energy and, if needed, can tap directly into your body energy to maintain power."

Patricia said, "That's interesting, Freddy, but why tap into the body energy?"

"A battery can run out. Even my energy packs can run

out, though it takes a long time. These belts will never run out of energy as long as the person wearing it is alive."

Patricia continued. "Freddy, say we are on a hostile planet. It's cold, and we have to travel a hundred miles to the pickup area. When we become tired and try to rest, won't these belts rape us of our energy to keep us warm? Therefore, we cannot ever rest."

"Patricia, by the way you used the word 'rape,' I feel that you are exceptionally worried about these belts causing you to become too tired to continue. Let me reassure you. If you were on a water planet, and it was two hundred degrees above the boiling point, and there was no air, and the gravity was ten times Earth normal, that underwater walk would be as simple as walking in the park. If you did become tired, then the belt would maintain a constant body temperature and Earth normal gravity. It would keep you dry, let you breathe, protect you from radiation, help you see in the dark, shield you from violence, and allow you to rest peacefully using only the wasted energy of your breathing. However, if you wish to have a backup power pack inserted into your belt, I will gladly do so. I do ask that you not use it unless absolutely necessary."

Susan asked, "So the army can use these to go down to the surface of unknown planets and do research without harm?"

"That's the plan, but these belts are not what I need tested the most."

Maggie asked, "What needs testing the most and why?"

"The helmets and armbands." I held up a helmet that looked like a standard flight helmet with communications and mirror visor.

Maggie repeated, "And why?"

"The helmet is for communication and has a really great heads-up display. The scanners in them can allow you a clear, unobstructed view, even in the deepest jungle. You can see underground, through ground, or around ground— your choice. Nice, don't you think?"

Maggie asked, "And the armband?"

"The ... um ... helmet can also transmit position and vital statistics to a command post so that the people in charge will know everything about you. Isn't that exactly what will be needed on new planets?"

Everyone that was looking at the small, stretchable, camouflaged armbands with the small black box built in, and several who were wearing them took them off and put them as far away from them as possible. Susan asked, "And the armbands?"

"Oh, they are only to be used after all the other equipment is fully tested and functional."

"Freddy, what do the armbands do?"

"They teleport you to any place you want to go within range. I hope."

Colleen grabbed my arm and yelled, "*You hope!*"

"Well ... I haven't had anybody crazy enough to agree to test them out until now."

Susan took my other arm, turned me around, and held up an armband. "These are untested transponding units?"

"Well ... yes."

Susan looked at the others and ordered, "Chief, I want every one of these armbands accounted for and stored back in their original crate. Then I want that crate sealed and sent back to the base and guarded."

I looked at Susan and asked, "Don't you think that you're going just a little bit too far? We teleport all the time. Besides, we don't even know if they work."

"No, Freddy, I don't think I am going too far. What would happen to the girl who used one that didn't work?"

"One of four things: nothing, did not move far enough, moved too far, or went in the wrong direction."

"'Nothing' and 'did not move far enough,' I can handle. But what does 'moved too far' mean?"

"Moved too far means she moved anywhere from a fraction of a millimeter to a thousand miles past where she wanted to go."

Susan was getting upset, and it was showing, "And what if she moved straight down or up one thousand miles past where she wanted to go, Freddy?"

I became annoyed and said, "Well, that's why she is wearing the survival belt and the communication helmet. Wherever she lands, we will know where she is and can retrieve her long before she is in any danger. I have equipment here that can lock onto her coordinates and bring her back, as long as she is willing to return. She will need to set her helmet to retrieval mode so that my transponder can fully identify her."

"And if she panics and teleports again before we can retrieve her?"

"Not to worry; she can only do that a couple of times before the power pack runs out. We'll retrieve her without a problem. Besides, the maximum distance she can move is a total of one thousand miles. An armband has limits, you know. Susan, I would really like to test the armbands, but it is not absolutely necessary this trip."

Susan looked at me and smiled. "I'll tell you what. I'll ask for volunteers, and if I get any, then we'll test them. Is that fair?"

I looked hopeful and said, "Sure."

Susan stood up and said, "Now listen up. Freddy wants to know if there is anyone aboard who is dumb enough to test his armband, knowing full well they could possibly end up God knows where and in unknown condition. If so, please stand up."

The two who were standing fought over the one seat nearest and ended up with one sitting in the other's lap. No one stood up. I put my hand on Susan's arm and said, "Let me try."

Susan sat down, and I stood up. "Let me rephrase that last request. I need a volunteer to test out a wonderful new machine. It's true that the person could possibly end up a little off course, and it's true that she may not be in an environment friendly to human life, but she will be wearing an untested belt that should take care of the issue. Any volunteers?" I used the most upbeat voice I could manage, but I heard heavy breathing and nothing else. I turned around, saying, "Well, I guess that's one we'll have to let the army test for us."

Susan said, "Good idea."

Denise yelled back from the cockpit, "Landing in three, two, one." She sat us down smoothly and quietly in the center of a large island in the South Pacific. The place chosen on the island was a valley with an open area large enough for the camp, with fresh running water and plenty of shade. The hatch opened, and the girls quickly became professional and scouted the area with scanners. Some had the helmets on and were using them to look around. The jungle was just that—an impressively tall, deep, dense mess of tangled vines, trees, and bushes, causing the floor to be nearly dark. Every bird—and there were a lot of them in every color of the rainbow—was screaming at us or yelling out warnings. One of the girls yelled back at the shuttle, "Hey, this helmet has infrared!"

I yelled out to her, "It has seven types of visuals. Choose the ones you like, and report if there are any issues." I had to yell, as the area was very noisy with all the birds upset.

I thought an island jungle would be quiet. Not so. It had all kinds of life, and everything seemed to make noise. The girls started clearing a place for the tents, and then tents went up quickly. Unpacking was accomplished within minutes. The cook was already starting lunch before I had my tent finished. My tent. I designed it myself. It was on a gravity sled, so I didn't have to lift a thing. Good thing too, as it weighs a ton. I touched the panel, and it followed me out of the shuttle. I picked a place and asked Susan, "Is this a good place to put my tent."

She said, "Yes, but ensure the front flap faces this way to keep the smoke from the cook fire out and allow for easy access."

I turned it around so the opening would face the way everyone else had theirs facing, and then I pressed the button. It immediately started unfolding. The looks I received from the girls said it all. When it finished unfolding, I had a nice little tent that was thirty feet wide, forty feet long, and ten feet high, with a front door, a rear door, two windows in the front and two on each side, a generator, powered lights, air conditioning, heating, the computer system, scanners, and pumps for water. I had to manually run the hose for the water, but now I had a working toilet and shower.

One of the girls came over and said, "I thought we were roughing it, Freddy."

I looked back and asked, "This isn't roughing it?" I went inside and set up the table and chairs. There were all kinds of bugs outside, and so I turned on the air for a nice positive air flow to keep flying insects out. Also, the air conditioning made it comfortable, as the temperature outside was easily in the nineties, and the humidity was horrible. I had plenty of work to do; I'd brought most of it with me in my portable tent.

Next, I checked the bedroom to ensure I remembered the linen, and then I checked the closet to ensure everything was still hanging up. Everything looked fine. I was in the walk-in closet when Susan came in.

"Freddy? Where are you?"

"I'm in the closet, checking my clothing."

She came around the corner with three of the team, looking disgusted. "Freddy, this looks just like your bedroom and office space back home. And it appears that you brought a lot of work with you."

"Yes. Nice, isn't it?"

Susan took my arm and led me outside. She said, "Go to it, girls."

I stood there in shock as the team took my clothes, toiletries, and my portable computer and placed them to the side. Then Susan said, "Freddy, close it up."

"Why?"

"Just do it."

I quickly ran inside and came out with two items, and then I reached over and pressed the button. It automatically shut down the generator, drained out the water, reeled in the hose, and folded up on itself. Within seconds, my tent was packed up and floating two feet above the ground, waiting for me to set it up. Colleen put a hand on it, and so it followed her back into the shuttle.

Susan pointed and asked, "What are those?"

"It's a hammock and my repair kit for the belts and helmets."

"Fine." Then she made a hand gesture, and a tarp, tent, and bedroll were dropped at my tent site. "You are here to rest and learn about nature. You are not spending all your time in a tent that is more like a luxury hotel, loaded down with work. I am sure you can figure out how to put this tent together, Freddy. Good luck." She went off to finish getting her nest in order.

It wasn't difficult to put the tent together properly. After all, I am somewhat intelligent. I simply watched Maggie put hers up and then did the same thing. I had the barbaric tent up in less than ten minutes. I also found a good place for the hammock and put it up. When I was finished, I went over and helped Julia put her tent up. She seemed to be getting frustrated. The team was going to put it up for her, but she insisted on doing it herself.

Aggie, Julia's mom, said, "When they said 'roughing it,' I did not think they truly meant roughing it!"

"Don't worry. You'll be well taken care of. Good food, clean water, that sort of thing, but don't expect a SEAL team to be gentle. You're guests, so you won't have to do any more than you want to. Me, I'm going to enjoy myself, do something of everything, go exploring, help in camp, go fishing, make a campfire, and check out all the life. This is going to be fun and very restful."

I guess my enthusiasm was helpful, as they both started relaxing and enjoying themselves. I heard a loud squawk and turned to see a colorful bird land in a tree nearby. I believe it's called a rainbow lorikeet—blue head, red beak, green back and wings, bright orange chest. I instinctively put my arm up and mentally called it to me. It flew down and perched on my arm. It weighed less than four ounces and was about eleven inches from top of head to tip of tail. I petted it and talked quietly to it as I checked it out. I had it open its wings so I could look underneath and check the wing span. When I was finished, and Julia had a chance to pet it, I rewarded it with a large insect that was slithering across Julia's foot and let it go. It took the insect and flew off into the nearest branch.

Julia said, "You just called her to you, and she came?"

"Almost. I use my mind to influence her into knowing that I will do her no harm, and then I let her know that she will be happy if she comes to me. I always reward the ones that do. It's their choice, you know. I would never force them into coming to me. That could be very traumatic for them. This one nests here and does not like us invading her space. I simply informed her that I would share all my insects with her. She is happy now."

"You can talk to animals?"

"Not really. But I can place ideas, pictures, feelings, and sometimes needs into their heads. At the same time, I can feel their emotions, needs, wants, and fears ... and I can calm them and know exactly how to treat them correctly. Specials like me are going to be very important during first contact with another sentient species. At least, there will be far fewer mistakes with specials helping."

Susan came over and said, "Double-check the zippers on your tents. Make sure they're fully zipped up and stay out of them as much as possible. There are a lot of insects in this area, and that way they won't be inside your tent when you go to bed tonight." Aggie, Julia, and I all rushed to our tents and checked the zippers. I went over to the shuttle, pulled out three belts, and walked back to Julia. I handed one to each and put one on myself, saying, "If you have a problem with bugs, simply ensure they are off you, and press the green button." I pressed it, and I was now fully shielded. Then I pressed it again, and I was unshielded. Julia pressed hers, and so did Aggie. Both left theirs on.

I had a great Idea and asked, "Julia, want to test out an armband?"

"No!"

Oh well. It was worth a try.

✦

Green said, "I'll test out an armband."

Red said, "So would I. However, I'd have a Purple test it first."

Black said, "Flying, teleporting, communications at a distance, automatic housing, and seeing in several modes. Don't you see? These are all ground troop support. We use these, except for the teleporting, in all our ground and ship-to-ship encounters."

Gray said, "I bet his are better than the pathetic things the Greens palm off on us. However, I don't like that 'vampire' idea. It sounds nasty. What is a vampire?"

Red said, "They have a bat they call a vampire. It is a flying mammal that eats insects. They also have a sect of humans that are vampires. They are few, and we have only caught two. They have a disease that causes them to need fresh blood. These were living off cattle. One bit a Green, and we had to kill the Green and the creature."

I thought, *Now that we have scanners, people are going to find them. Besides, I can fix that with my AD.*

Little Yellows must have picked up my thoughts. "We do not believe that the rest of the humans know about the vampires. This one was thinking he can fix the disease with his AutoDoctor."

Red came over to me and asked, "Little Red, can your AutoDoctor fix any disease? Can you program it to heal our kind?"

I reached up a hand and touched one Little Yellow, reading her entire body. "Yes."

Red turned and said to the Body Proper, "This race is needed desperately and as friends, not slaves. When are our reinforcements arriving? We may need to show them that we can and will win this war unless they agree to an unconditional surrender."

A voice came through Little Yellows, saying, "We will inform His Majesty, though he is not in the mood at this time to listen. A Great Ship is on the way and will be here in eighteen hands. At that time, he is going to transfer to the Great Ship. He is fully planning to destroy this species as they have embarrassed him by destroying half our fleet."

I asked the great computer intelligence on this ship, "Body Proper, when are my reinforcements arriving?"

"Which wave?"

I smiled. "Tuned into our communications, I see. I'll let them know. The first and second wave, please."

"The first wave is due in one hand; the second will arrive in sixteen hands, or hours, in your terms."

"Thank you."

All the colors were looking at me.

Red asked, "He can communicate with the Body Proper?"

Little Yellows said, "Not really. The Body Proper was communication through us, and so he was attuned."

Red looked relieved. "I am glad that was all. Green, please continue."

I smiled and thought, *Little did they know. I warned the fleet about the Great Ship.*

CHAPTER 27

✦ ✦ ✦

TAMPERING

After lunch, Susan had the team assembled in belts and helmets and set them to exploring the island. Everyone in camp wore belts and helmets, including Julia and Aggie. Even the cook was wearing them. I asked Susan why.

Susan said, "If they are stuck in an unfriendly place, then they will know they can do the simple things like cooking, eating, cleaning, mending, sleeping, and standing watch. Everyone will be wearing constantly and will be observed by us at the base. I am very glad to see that Aggie and Julia are wearing and using the survival belts already."

"Thanks, but that was to help them with bugs. Julia and Aggie are wearing perfume. The bugs really like them."

Susan smiled. "Yes, they would. I'll try to school them about camping. They don't need helmets as long as we are watching them with scanners."

"Say, there is nothing poisonous, like snakes and spiders, is there?"

"No. I researched the place. There are a lot of dangers here." She looked around as if to emphasize all around us and then added, "But nothing deadly. The terrain is the biggest problem. You could be walking through the forest and walk right off a cliff or fall down a hole. Be careful."

"I will."

"Good. Tomorrow we'll go fishing, and I'll teach you everything I know. Which isn't much, but Chief Donet will be able to help more in that area."

"Speaking of Betsy Donet, do you think it was wise to send her off alone? I mean, no offense, but I wouldn't allow her in my shop without major supervision. She's a klutz."

"Remember what she majored in?"

"Um ... forestry?"

"That's correct. It's true she is a klutz at home but not here. This is her love. This is her normal environment. Here, she is home."

Susan walked over to talk with Julia and Aggie, so I picked up a command helmet to listen in.

Colleen said, "This is command. Who just came online?"

"I did, Colleen."

"Very well, Freddy. Listen in, but keep quiet. Test three, Henderson! Come down from there!"

Chief Patricia Henderson yelled out, "This is test three. I can fly, Colleen. I can actually fly. It's wonderful."

I checked where she was and could see and feel that Colleen was having problems with Patricia flying so high. Patricia was over twenty-five kilometers up and climbing. I put a hand on Colleen's arm and said, "Patricia, I know that flying is fun, but you have left the troposphere and entered the stratosphere, and you are quickly heading toward the mesosphere. You're making people nervous. Please come down."

"Oh, very well."

Scanners showed her returning, so I left it at that. To reassure Colleen, I said, "The belt should work fine out in space, but it is not tested there yet. No sense taking chances."

She toggled the private switch and said, "I agree, Freddy." She placed the switch back into command mode and ordered, "Report."

"Lieutenant Uniceson reports all's well. The system is working as advertised plus."

"Chief Darnel reports all's well. System working 100 percent. You would not believe—"

Colleen broke in. "Keep the chatter down! Continue reports."

"Chief Henderson reports all's well. System working at 100 percent."

"Chief Swanson reports all's well. System working 100 percent."

"Chief Donet reports all's well. Um ... I'll turn the system on now."

Colleen broke in again. "Betsy, we are not here for your entertainment. Use the system, and test it out completely. Continue reports." There was some snickering in the background from several of the girls.

"Petty Officer Smith reports all's well. System working at 100 percent."

"Petty Officer Parks reports all's well. System helmet working 100 percent. Belt not working. I'm stuck on the top of the mountain. It's a nice view."

Colleen said, "Stay there, and we'll send you a backup belt."

Maggie Parks retorted in a lazy tone, "Oh"—big yawn—"I'm not going anywhere."

Colleen frowned and ordered, "Chief Henderson. Repeat: Patricia, return to camp and pick up a replacement belt for Maggie. Her belt is out, and she is stuck on the top of the mountain. She is in good condition but getting drowsy for some reason. I want her escorted back here immediately."

"This is Chief Henderson, on my way, Colleen."

Colleen ordered, "Continue reports."

"Petty Officer Denise Potter reports all's well. System working 100 percent. I am headed up the mountain to check on Maggie. Will report if any issues."

"Petty Officer Pendelson reports all's well. System working 100 percent. I am also headed toward the mountain."

I placed a hand on Colleen's arm and whispered, "One belt can carry two or three people, if she is truly drowsy."

Colleen ordered, "Petty Officer Potter. Repeat: Denise. Freddy tells me that the belts can carry two or three people. New orders. Pick up Maggie and bring her back to camp. Dorothy Pendelson, give escort."

"This is Denise. Understood."

"This is Dorothy. Understood."

"This is Patricia. Understood. Will report to command post and await orders."

Colleen turned to me and said, "I'm sure that Maggie is doing well, but please check her when she returns."

"I will."

"Good. The helmets are wonderful. Well thought out. Each one allows for complete silence, talk with command only, private with any other helmet, background chatter so you can hear what's going on, notification when a channel is open, and emergency override to command on all helmets. We're practicing not using the normal commands like 'over and out' just to see if it all works, and it does. Saves a lot of time if we know who is keyed up and ready to talk and who is not. Also, we know if two are keyed at the same time. Helps us know when a message was transmitted. And I love the wait-in-line mode. You key up and can't transmit until you get a green light that tells you you're connected. As command, I know how many people want to talk to me, and I can pick and choose which ones are priority. Right now, everything is quiet, but Maggie and Denise have priority as a possible emergency."

I placed a hand on her arm. "See this readout. Maggie is doing fine, though she is tired for some reason. Her energy is slightly drained."

"Yes, and that's why I haven't pulled in the big guns. I could easily have three ships here in a second to pull her out. We are not putting anyone in danger this time out. This is simply a test run of equipment."

"Good."

"I can see your worry, Freddy. Don't worry. Relax. We'll keep you informed." She gently pulled the helmet off my head and motioned for me to relax.

I went over to the hammock and started swinging a little. When Maggie came down, she was sound asleep in Denise's arms. Denise brought her directly to me. Julia and Aggie were shocked and worried.

I examined her. "There is nothing wrong with her except that her energy is very low. She'll sleep it off in an hour or two. She may have a slight headache when she wakes."

Susan asked, "What went wrong, Freddy?"

"I won't know until I look at the belt." I took the belt off her and opened up the electronics. I smiled, reached in, and removed a tiny screwdriver. I looked up at Susan, laughing, "Maggie is what went wrong."

Susan frowned, "Explain, please."

"You give an electronics toy to an electronics genius, and what happens? She pulls it apart to see how it works." I held up the screwdriver and said, "See this? She shorted out the energy pack, and the belt used her body to replace the lost energy, which fried the energy input circuits as it gathered energy too quickly. Design flaw that is easily fixed. Please tell everyone that Maggie is the first to find a flaw. Congratulate her. Then chew her out for tampering, please."

Susan was just a little upset that Maggie tampered with the equipment and caused issues. She didn't show it, but

I could feel it. I was fairly sure Maggie was going to find herself on kitchen patrol for the rest of the trip.

Susan ordered, "Colleen, tell everyone what happened, and let them know I'll fry the next one that tampers with the equipment!"

Julia had her hands resting on the belt, and she quickly took them off.

Colleen toggled the all-hands switch and ordered, "Attention, team. Maggie will be okay. She is just very tired. She tampered with the circuits of the belt and caused the belt to need to reenergize quickly. Being vampire in nature, you can guess from where the belt took the energy. Orders are, don't tamper with any of the equipment. In addition, it's time, and the cook is nearly finished making dinner. Everyone report and return."

I couldn't hear what was going on, but I could see Colleen marking off each person as they reported on a small board and marking them a second time as they showed up. It's good working with professionals. Far fewer worries.

✦

Red said, "Well, Gray, now we know what vampire means. It takes your energy away if it needs energy to keep you alive."

Green said, "With the communications and the readouts on personal vital signs, everyone will quickly know if there is a problem. We can do that, but Gray said not to clutter things up."

Gray said rather disinterestedly, "Who cares if someone is not doing well? Leave him, and continue with the plan."

I said, "Fool!" at the same time Little Yellows whispered to herself, "Fool!" We both started laughing. Big Yellows and

Green caught what happened and were laughing. Gray was getting mad.

Gray asked in a tone that screamed warning, "What did it say about me this time?"

Little Yellows said, "It is not what he said that we are laughing about. It is the fact that he and we said the same thing at the same time. We think a lot alike."

Red said, "Amazing. You actually said the same thing at the same time. What did you say?"

"Fool!"

Gray took a step forward and said, "You had better be careful, Yellows."

A Black stepped up and turned toward Gray. "Do you have a death wish, little Gray."

Gray quickly backed down. "No."

Six tentacles shot into—not around but into—Gray and picked him up. He was screaming in pain. "No, what?"

"No, Great One. I did not mean to offend."

The tentacles pulled out so quickly that I could not see the move. As the Black turned and started back to his position, Gray fell from the ceiling to the floor with a bang. He picked himself up and left.

No one said a word for several seconds.

Blue finally broke the stillness and said, "Body Proper, watch that Gray. He may wish revenge."

Body Proper answered, "I would close the doors as he is returning with a blasting weapon."

Gray walked back in. The weapon was still at his side. His hand was on it, but he did not draw the weapon. He said, "If you attack me again, you had better kill me." He turned my way without taking his eyes off the others. "Say something about me again, and see if you are not expendable."

I reached out with my mind, and his weapon became

white hot. He tried to pull it but it was now melted into the holder.

Black walked over and said, "Body Proper, we need a new Gray. Have any been watching?"

"*Several.*"

"Please send one now." He turned to another Black. "Take this one to the Black pens, and let them play with him."

Gray left in the arms of a big Black. Gray was begging, "No! No! Not that! I'll be quiet. I'll be good. Not the pens!" His voice trailed off.

Little Yellows said to me. "Now, how did you make his weapon hot, little one?"

Red said, "He tampered again. Bring me a dampening helmet."

A Green brought over a big device that looked like a metal helmet enclosure of some sort. They transferred it into the tank and placed it over my head. My mental powers shut off. Darn!

Red said, "Continue, Green."

✦ ✦ ✦

CHAPTER 28

TESTING

I was swinging in the hammock when Julia came over.

"Hi, Freddy."

"Hi, Julia. Want to swing? There is plenty of room."

"Okay."

I stopped the swing, and she climbed on, and I started the swing again." Susan was at the command post, going over the reports, and Aggie was sitting in front of her tent, picking bugs off her pants. Both gave me a funny look.

Julia noticed and said, "I don't think they want us together much. Mother doesn't because you're always in some danger. Why not Susan?"

"Susan does not like ruffles and lace. She wants me around someone strong and fast."

"Are you attracted to someone strong and fast, or are you more ruffles and lace?"

"Actually, I've been too busy to give it much thought."

"Don't start skirting around issues. Which is it?"

"I'm really not avoiding the issue. It's just that ..."

"What?"

"Being empathic and telepathic, I find myself drawn toward females who have good minds. I would have to say intelligence and order inside a mind is the first thing that draws my attention."

She sadly said, "I had not thought of that. I suppose only specials have that kind of mind."

"Absolutely not. That's not even close to being correct. Specials are not special when it comes to intelligence. We have some remarkable specials at home, and believe me, they would test out as totally normal for intelligence."

"Then what makes a person intelligent?"

"I am not really sure what made them different at birth. However, what makes them different when they reach my age is what they have done with their lives. For instance, you have a great mind."

"I do?"

"Yes. If you took the proper tests, I am sure you would come out well above normal. Now, what got you to that point? Do you like to read?"

"Yes, I love to read."

"I would also bet you read a lot, and that increases your knowledge and helps organize your brain. In addition, you are a good student, aren't you?"

"Four point zero, all the way."

"Highly expected with a good mind like yours. You read, you study, you work at life, and therefore, you make your mind work." I turned to her. "And that's what makes a mind intelligent and ordered. Putting it to work and exercising the mind makes you the person you are."

"That's nice of you to say, Freddy."

"I won't lie to you, Julia. When I say you have a good mind—an attractive mind—I mean just that. I am not saying I am attracted to you. Just that you are attractive because of your mind."

"And once you get past the mind and see the girl?"

"Then I would have to say health."

"Health?"

"Does she care enough to keep herself healthy?"

"Oh, now were talking looks."

"In a way but not what you're thinking. I have seen some very lovely girls that are not healthy and some homely girls that are very healthy. The prettiest girl I have ever seen wears glasses and has a mole on her chin."

She reached over and pushed my shoulder. "You're joking."

"No. What made her pretty is that when I touched her hand, there was nothing to heal. Nothing to fix that was caused by her. Her hair was well taken care of, and her teeth were clean, and she was clean. She exercised, and her body showed it, in that her muscles were tight and lean. However, her mind was unorganized and weak."

"Then strong and fast is important?"

"No. Strong and fast is normally healthy, but you can be healthy without being strong and fast. We had a girl called Tammy at home for a while. She had a great mind, and she was very healthy, small, weak, and almost fragile. I was very attracted to her, and so was every man at home. She had a special ability that drove men crazy in need for her. However, she was not strong or fast."

"You talk of her in the past tense. What happened to her?"

"Becky happened. My love for Becky let me see through Tammy's special ability, and I sent Tammy away until she could control her special ability. We called it Tammy-craving. She'll be okay once she figures out how to control it."

"You love Becky a lot, don't you?"

"It's kind of strange. I would do almost anything for her. I think of her more than anything else. However, we don't seem to hit it off too well when we're together."

"Rocky relationship?"

"Aren't all relationships rocky?"

"I'd have to agree on that. You're not watching what you say with me. Why? I could report in the magazine that you have a rocky relationship with Becky."

"Go ahead."

"You don't mind?"

"I'm not one to hide anything except my inventions. I am who I am. I don't understand why you are interested in me. Why the fan club?"

She looked over at me with a smile, patted my check, and said, "You really don't know, do you?"

"No. So why?"

She stopped the swing and got off.

"Hey, I answered your questions, Julia!"

As she was walking away she looked back at me with a smile and said, "Thank you."

I wanted to say more, but as soon as Julia walked away, the team was on me, wanting to talk about the belt and helmet.

Lieutenant Uniceson was the first to reach me. "Freddy, these are great. Too bad about Maggie, but I had a great time. There seems to be several controls I can't activate. The rest of the girls say the same thing."

I took my eyes off Julia, the brat, and focused on the lieutenant. I reached over and touched her arm. "I have them deactivated at this time, sir."

"Why?"

"For safety reasons. I need you to be fully used to what I have activated before I can allow the use of the rest of the system."

"What do they do?"

I smiled at that. "Tell you in about a week."

"Freddy, you do love to keep people in suspense." She hit my arm in a friendly manner and had to grab the swing to keep me from falling out. "You need to loosen up this swing. It's too tight."

Katie and Marian made it to me next, but the lieutenant warned them, "He's not telling. Wants us to use 'em for a week and become fully comfortable with 'em before allowing us the full use."

Katie looked at me with a critical eye, saying to the lieutenant, "I'll get Julia to jiggle it out of him."

I reached out and touched Katie and then Marian, and I retorted, "Fat chance, you two."

Marian smiled. "What's the matter, Freddy? Julia and you seem to be getting along really well. That was a nice touch, having her swing with you. Very romantic."

"Romantic! She was here just long enough to get the information she wanted without telling me anything I wanted to know. Then she left to go write it down. She could be writing anything!"

Patricia walked up and said, "Lay off, you two. Freddy is supposed to be enjoying his time off. Nice job with the belt and helmet, but there seem to be controls I can't activate. What's the deal?"

I looked at the lieutenant, waiting for her to speak up, but she just stared back. I took hold of Patricia's arm and said, "Patricia, I don't wish to have to tell everyone individually, so I'll talk about the other controls after dinner. Okay?"

"Sure, I can wait. See you after dinner, Freddy." She turned to walk away.

The lieutenant said, "You'll be waiting to hear he's not telling."

She stopped, turned around, and started walking back. The look on her face said I was about to tell whether I wanted to or not.

Susan walked over and put a hand on her arm. "Stop right there."

Patricia stopped but said, "This isn't over, Freddy."

Susan looked at Patricia and said, "No, it's not over." Then she turned to me. "Freddy."

I gave her the most innocent look I could achieve. "Yes."

"Don't use those big eyes on me, young man! When you hold back information about ships and projects, I get upset, but I don't push too hard. This time we are field testing your equipment. We need to understand the full capabilities, or the testing is over. Do you understand?"

I could feel she was quite serious, so I touched Susan's arm and said, "Come here, Patricia, and give me your belt." She took it off and handed it to me. I went into my tent and came back out with the repair kit, opened it up, and turned on the computer. I opened the belt and took out the electronic pack, plugged it into the computer, and reprogrammed it so that it had all capabilities. While I was reprogramming, I explained. "The belts are for moving and working in hostile environments. Whether out in space or on some forbidden planet, these belts will protect you from almost everything. The shielding they provide will allow you to withstand temperatures from -273 degrees Celsius, or absolute zero, to above 25,000 degrees Celsius. I placed tools inside them to help with repairs and help you survive." I put the belt back together and handed it to Patricia. "Here." I started putting my repair kit back.

She put the belt on rather reluctantly and looked into her helmet's display. "Everything seems to be available now, Captain."

Susan ordered, "Toggle through, and see what you have."

"Wait! Wait, wait, wait!" I said. "Don't do a thing until I say. I don't want to be killed."

"Killed?"

I think everyone in the camp, including Julia and Aggie, said killed at the same time.

Sounding a little apologetic, I said, "Yes, well, killed is maybe a little strong. How about cut in half?" Susan picked me up and sat me gently in the swing. Then she put an arm on each side of me so she could look me right in the face. I teleported to the other side of the lieutenant. "Now look, you want me to explain or not?"

Betsy tapped me on the head, saying, "Please go ahead." I didn't even see her until she tapped me. One second she wasn't in the camp, and in the next she was beside me. It startled me, and I teleported over to Colleen.

"Don't hide behind me, Freddy." Colleen grabbed my arm and pulled me out from behind her.

Susan said, "Stop teleporting, Freddy! Tell us what the other capabilities are."

"Okay, okay. Calm down." I'm not sure if I was saying that to them as much as I was saying it to myself. "Patricia?"

"Yes."

"Toggle to 'stealth' mode."

"Very well." She did so and instantly disappeared.

Susan asked, "Where did she go?"

"I'm right here, Captain." Those who still had their helmets on could hear Patricia very clearly. No one else could hear anything Patricia said or did.

The lieutenant ordered, "Everyone, helmets back on."

Susan put her helmet on and toggled through all the sight modes and found Patricia on several different modes.

I went into lecturing mode. "As you can see—or not see, whichever—in the stealth mode Patricia is completely invisible to the unaided eye. In addition, she can talk, walk, run, whatever, and she won't make any noise. Scanners will pick her up, and so do four of the seven modes of seeing in the helmets. The helmet will send her voice to other helmets, but no one else can hear her. The entire team could walk into a movie, sit in the back, and yell at each other, and no one else would ever know. If we're moving people out to other planets, I am sure that the passengers will be a lot less nervous if they don't see people working on the outside of the ship. Aren't you?"

Patricia said, "This is amazing."

Susan said, "Freddy, please continue."

"Patricia, please come out of stealth mode so we can see you." She did. "Now toggle on 'beam.'"

She did, and her shield changed to a red color. "How are you feeling, Patricia?"

"I'm fine. Why the color change in my shield?"

Betsy was now near me, so I touched her arm. I looked at Patricia and said, "The color change is to warn you that you have the laser armed. Point at the log over there." She pointed to the log. "Now toggle 'long beam' and then 'on,' and slice that log in two." She did, and a beam shot out, putting a hole through the log and into the ground. She moved her finger, and the beam cut the log into two parts. "Now, toggle to 'off,' and place it in short beam.

"Done."

"You can probably use that five or six times before the belt will need recharging. If there was a power pack added to the belt, then you could do it all day. Last but not least, toggle on 'TBG,' or tractor beam gun," The shield became light blue. "Point at the section you just cut off. Lift it with your mind. Very good. Now bring it here, and set it down for a stool." The section of log floated through the air, flipped to the ends, and sat gently down. "Doing that once should be no problem. If you do that more than once without a power-pack backup, you would be so tired you would drop where you stand.

Patricia toggled off TBG and removed her helmet. "That's amazing, and it was all done off my own power?"

"Mostly your own wasted body energy. But when you go into the TBG or beam modes, you start using up more than wasted energy. It's best to have a power pack to use for those modes."

Susan asked, "Will our wasted energy recharge the power packs?"

"Sure."

"Then I would prefer that the belts have that power pack to use. Then when we rest, we can recharge the pack and start out fully charged."

"I agree, Susan, but right now, I want to test out the belt without the extra power. I need to see the effect it has in the human body, if any."

Colleen asked, "If any? What about Maggie?"

"Maggie did that to herself. Have you noticed that I have been touching each of you when I did not need to?"

"Yes."

"I'm monitoring your vital signs and your energy, protein, and fat use—everything that your body is burning up and will need replaced. So far, everything looks normal, but we need to give it a little time to see if there are any long-term effects."

Julia said, "That's why you touched my arm? Sweet, I'm a guinea pig."

I looked over at Julia and said, "You don't have to test the equipment, but there will be a lot of young adults moving to my new home on Mars, and they will need to know that these belts work for them. You're doing them a big favor."

The cook yelled out, "Dinner!" So we all headed toward the food. Something about camping makes me hungry. I'll have to research that.

During dinner and over the next couple of days, it came

up several times that the belt was a nice assassin's tool. Julia and Aggie came to me to talk about it.

✦

The new Gray said, "They have these for their ground troops?"

Red said, "Count on it."

Gray thought for a second. I received the opinion that this Gray was different.

Gray finally said, "Are we thinking of taking over their planet?"

Blue said, "That was the idea."

Black said, "As new information is coming in, we are revising our plans accordingly."

Gray said, "Expected, Great One. Your kind is not one for wasting our color. Still, this will make it difficult. Our hand weapons will not penetrate their shields."

I said to Little Yellows, who was still holding me, "Liar."

Little Yellows said, "Gray, he does not believe you. Your predecessor carried in a weapon that could reach through the shields."

Gray said, "The fool." Then he went back to thinking.

Red asked, "What is going through your mind, Admiral?"

I said to myself, "So that's it. This one was their genius admiral, and I already told him I knew his hand weapons worked against my body shields. I worked with Susan long enough to know these types. Any little bit of information pulled out in any way will help them. Time to be quiet."

The Gray said, "Then he knows our weapons will breach his ships' shields." No one said anything. He looked at Little Yellows.

Little Yellows said, "He said and thought nothing."

Gray said matter-of-factly, "Good, then they do." Then he looked at Little Yellows, waiting for a response.

Little Yellows said, "I received nothing, Admiral."

Gray said, "Green, please continue. Perhaps we can get some reaction when we read his memories."

Green said, "As you wish, Admiral."

C H A P T E R   2 9

✦ ✦ ✦

TOOLS

Aggie asked, "Freddy, do you have a minute?"

"Sure, Aggie. Hi, Julia. What's up?"

"Have you heard what the team is talking about lately? They're calling your belt the 'assassin's belt.'"

"Typical."

Julia became a little hot. "Why are you making these things for them?"

I knew this argument was going to come up, so I prepared for it. Goodness knows I argued this out with myself often enough. "Now Julia, if I made a toy for a two-year-old, these girls would find a deadly use for it. Sure, the belt can be used for assassins' work, but so is a glass cutter, and that is not what it was designed for. Watch." I got up from the log stool and opened my repair kit. I pulled out a small hand ax. "Do you know what this is?"

Aggie answered while putting a hand on Julia's mouth. "It's a hatchet. Used every day by woodsmen."

"True, but note the power supply in the handle. When I turn it on, it vibrates and becomes a super-hatchet. Watch." I walked over to the log and, in one whack, cut a two-foot piece off the end. I used my abilities to levitate it in the air and bring it back over to where they were. I set it down as a second stool. "This is a lazy person's hatchet."

Summer saw me cut the log and came over. "Can I see that?" I handed it to her. "Nice; this could cut right through standard armor and split a man in two." She walked off with it to test it out.

I yelled to her, "I want that back when you're done!" Then I turned to Julia and said, "See what I mean?"

"Yes. So most of the things you build are not weapons?"

"Of course not. Look. I built a ship to bring in materials from the asteroid belt. The ship has lasers to cut the asteroid into manageable chunks. It has a beam that agitates and makes the molecules fly apart so that you can pick out the metals you need, and it has a tractor beam strong enough to pull in all the material. The shields are extra strong in case the materials accidentally hit the ship. Beautiful design. You know it as the shark-class ship called the Razor."

"But that was the most fearsome ship in the war!"

"Exactly. I didn't build it for war. And it is actually being used to pull materials from the asteroid belt with a lot of success. But anything and everything I build is used by the military first, and they have a different set of minds than you and me. I started out trying not to have government influence in my projects. However, I could not build the ES *Protectress* fast enough to save the world without their help, so I allowed it. Then bad people started paying way too much attention to me, and I needed the government's protection. Then the war started, and again we all needed the government's help. I had to give them all the ships. Things never work out the way I planned them."

Aggie patted my arm and said, "I'm sorry, Freddy."

I added, "I used to cry myself to sleep, thinking about the people that could be harmed. I don't anymore. I design, build, and show it to the military. They take all responsibility for how it is used. Not long ago, my AD was used to help disguise a man so that he could become president. Should I not have invented the AutoDoc?"

Julia answered, "No. That was a great invention. People love you for it."

"Yet it is being used to harm people. When the IC chip was invented, it led to portable computers, cell phones, and thousands of things we use every day. Do you think the inventor envisioned it being used for guidance systems for missiles? I think not, and I don't think it would be appropriate to hold Intel or Motorola responsible for the way IC chips are used. I've thought about this long and hard. It comes to this: I need to invent. I want to see people make it to other worlds, and I want to visit other worlds. I am going to invent things that get us there and allow us to stay as safe as possible. Others will find other uses for my equipment. Can't be helped. But that should not slow me down."

Aggie said, "Looking at it that way and thinking about it, you're right. It does not matter what you invent. The military will turn it into a weapon. However, you are making progress toward colonizing other worlds."

"And in such, I'm making a better world for all of us."

Julia kissed my cheek really quick before I could pull away. "I like that." She started writing in her notepad—"A better world for all of us."

I jumped up and yelled, "Summer!" and then teleported to her side. I grabbed the stump where her hand used to be and stopped the bleeding. Then I asked, "Where did it go?"

"It's over there." Using her one remaining hand, she pointed to a spot on the ground.

I walked her over to the spot and picked it up. Julia and Aggie were running up, along with several of the team. Without thinking, I handed the hand to Julia and said, "Wash this off, please."

Julia fainted. Aggie caught her. Maggie took the hand and ran over to the small waterfall. When she returned, I reattached the hand to the arm and healed it. "You know the drill, Summer. There'll be little to no use of that hand until the mending hardens up. Three days hand rest for you. And next time I let you play with one of my toys, you have to have adult supervision." Everyone laughed, including Summer. Aggie was smiling, and Julia was just coming around.

"Where's the hand? Oh, Freddy. I'm sorry."

Aggie said, "The hand was washed off and reattached. With Freddy here to do healing, the girls are not in danger." Julia picked up her pen and notepad and said, "Mom, tell me everything. I want to know each detail."

They walked off, and Summer said quietly. "Not the girl for you, Freddy. Not if she faints at the first sign of blood."

"I already knew that. If Becky were here, she would have picked up the hand before I did and started washing it off without needing to be told."

"You don't know that for sure, Freddy." She ruffled my hair. "You're blind with love, boy."

"Yes, I suppose I am. I'll have to test it sometime. Want to cut your hand off for me on cue this time?"

"No!"

"Darn. I'll just have to wait until something comes up."

✦

Gray said, "She cut her hand off without a word or scream. He attached it, and she said nothing. Are all their military that strong?"

Red said, "We picked up few military. The ones we did pick up were stubborn. Luckily, their minds are easy to probe."

Gray said, "And this one's mind—is it easy to probe?"

Red said proudly, "This one is their top Red. Probing is difficult. We are barely getting what we have now. We have allowed him to think and work on escaping so that he would allow us to probe as much as we have. He did not know about the dampening helmet."

Gray said, "Tricky, Red. I like you. So that is why you allowed him to cause all that trouble."

Black said, "I was wondering that at first. When I figured it out, I was upset that Gray kept doing things to cause this creature to give away what he was doing."

Gray said, "I watched the foolishness of my pen mate with distaste. I am sorry for his stupidity. However, I have little in my pen to work with. He is a good one for special projects, and I would like him back in one piece, please. I learned much watching the banter."

Black made a motion to another, and that one left.

Green said, "May I start before he closes up entirely? He is trying to shut me out."

Gray said, "Yes, please continue."

Red said, "One thing first. Gray, what did you think about his warning?"

Gray said, "I took it seriously. This is the first race to give us trouble besides the undead and machines. We can ill afford a third front.

Black said, "Green, please."

✦ ✦ ✦

EMPATHY

The next day everyone was out testing the equipment except Petty Officer Parks. She had camp cleanup, including latrine duty. Susan, the cook, Aggie, and Julia were also in camp. Julia and Aggie were miserable. Even with the special equipment, they were constantly attacked by bugs. Poor Julia was even attacked by the birds.

Susan came to me with two fishing poles and said, "Freddy, it's time to teach you something about fishing and camping."

I grabbed my helmet and said, "Great, let's go. Anything to get away from Julia's screaming and complaining."

Julia and Aggie grabbed their helmets and came with us. Julia asked, "Where we going?"

Susan answered, "We are going fishing. Betsy found a little pond only a few hundred feet from here that she says has lots of fish. I am going to teach Freddy how to catch fish."

Aggie asked, "May we tag along?"

Susan smiled and, in her lecturing tone, said, "I hoped you would. I would like to give all three of you some pointers on camping." We started heading down from the camp.

"Now the first thing you should understand about camping is that bugs, birds, wolves, bears, men, and all kinds of pests can smell. Some pests, you don't want to attract."

Julia said, "Like bugs."

Susan continued. "Yes, like bugs. Bugs love flowers. The reason they are attracted to flowers is what? Aggie?"

"I would guess the sweet smell."

"Correct, and what else?"

"The way flowers look."

"Close. It's the colors. Certain bugs are attracted to specific colors and smells, like a young boy to the smell and look of a barbecue. Example: that nice yellow dress Julia is wearing with the bright white ruffles looks just like a flower to half the bugs and birds in this jungle."

Aggie said, "That's why Julia was dive-bombed several times by a bird this morning, and the bugs are constantly following her."

Susan answered, "Sort of. The bugs are following her because she is the best food source in the jungle. She smells just like a flower and looks like a gigantic flower, and it makes them hungry. Some bugs, like the praying mantis she screamed about this morning, are looking to eat those bugs. Therefore, where is the best place to find dinner for the bug-eating bugs?"

I answered, "On the flower?"

"Exactly! The bird was trying to eat some of the bugs that were attracted to you, as climbing on you put them out in the open and made them easy pickings."

Julia said, "That's not fair!"

Aggie said, "Who ever told you life is fair!" She turned to Susan and asked, "So you're saying that we are bringing this on ourselves by wearing sweet-smelling perfume and other toiletries?"

Susan smiled. "Try washing your entire body, including

hair, in nonperfumed soap and then dressing in non–bright green, dark brown, and dark grays, and see what happens. Another issue: Julia takes a lot of notes. There are two issues with this. First, we are testing equipment. If any mention is made toward what equipment we are testing and its uses or effects at any time by anyone, you will never see Freddy again—ever."

Julia turned hostile. "That has to be the umpteenth time you told me that."

"I understand that, so please explain why your notes include the armband, belt, and helmet you are wearing. Oh, I almost forgot—and the vibrating ax. I noticed you didn't say anything about fainting."

"How did you know that?"

"I can go invisible. Remember?"

"That's not fair. Besides, no one will ever get those notes."

"You're right. They are being burned as we speak."

Julia tried to turn around and go back to camp, but Susan reached out, picked her up, and placed her back on course for the pond. "We're going fishing. The second issue is that you use bright pink paper and scented ink."

Julia's eyes widened, "That's why the bugs are always climbing up on my notepad!"

Susan said, "Correct. Your notepads are being replaced with marine-issue standard green pads and pens that don't have scented ink, like bubblegum and cherry. Where did you get that junk?"

Julia became defensive. "Any good office supply store."

Susan's smile widened. "Good. I was worried that there was a camping store out there that was selling that stuff. It is apparent that you did not come prepared for camping. We are helping you so that you can enjoy this trip and so that you don't hurt your voice—and our ears—with all that screaming. All your clothing and toiletries are being replaced with standard-issue military. Everything you brought is being replaced with items that are better suited for camping. When we return, you will take a bath and wash off the stench of that perfume, and the clothes you are wearing now will be packed away."

Aggie said with genuine appreciation, "Thank you."

Julia stubbornly said, "And if I refuse?"

Susan's smile vanished. "Then you will be given a bath and left to dress or not dress, your choice."

I said, "I think I'll take a walk when we return. I don't want to be around for that."

Aggie said to Julia, "Child! It's going to be a horrible two weeks if we have to spend the entire time swatting bugs as big as my fist. The captain is doing us a big favor. Now you apologize."

"I'm sorry. I will comply with this. But I don't like people going through my notes."

Susan very sternly said, "You had better take good notes and tell the whole truth because we have everything you have done so far on scanning record, including this walk. We can show the world the truth—the fainting, the screaming. You could become the biggest laughing stock on the face of the planet."

I looked up at Susan and said worriedly, "I don't think that will be necessary."

Susan stopped and turned to me. "Julia is showing signs of becoming a bad reporter—the kind that changes the facts to make things look her way. I won't have that kind of person around my son!"

Everyone was shocked. Susan turned and walked toward the pond. It was several minutes before the silence was broken.

Julia said, "You wouldn't happen to have one of

those military-issue pads and pens with you right now. Would you?"

Susan smiled, reached into her pack, and said, "As a matter of fact." She handed Julia a pad and pen.

All I said was, "Darn. I wasn't going to tell her she forgot hers."

Susan smiled. "That's okay. I wasn't going to tell her that the reason she was allowed to come along on this fishing trip is that we need bait, and that dress will attract all kinds of bugs we can use."

For the first time, Julia turned red. I thought, *This is great.* Problem was, Julia saw my smile. The look she gave me said, *"Just you wait!"* But what she said was, "Freddy, could you please adjust my belt so I can go invisible?"

I seriously answered, "To do that I would have to give you the TBG and laser also. I don't have it on mine, and you don't get it on yours. Besides, I doubt your mother would allow me to give you those abilities."

Aggie said sternly, "No, she would not!"

We reached the pond, and unbeknownst to Julia, Susan had already picked several large bugs off her back and hair and one from my hair. I asked Susan, "You wouldn't have packed some camping stuff for me also, would you? Especially nonperfumed shampoo?"

Susan said, "Yours is all being changed out also. I am sorry. I should have schooled you on camping a long time ago. There is much you need to learn about roughing it. When you go out to other worlds, you will need to know things that others have taken decades to learn. We can teach you, but it will take a few months."

"I need to learn, Mother."

"I know."

The pond wasn't very big—about eighty feet across and situated at the bottom of a twenty-foot waterfall that seemed to float over the edge in a three-foot area and crash into the pond. It looked like a good place to swim. We set up on a rock outcropping, and Susan went through how to prepare the fishing pole and put the bait on the hook. I cringed when she stabbed the insect, and I put my shields up. I don't care what some people think. Insects do have feelings! But nothing prepared me for catching a fish. The fish bit, and I pulled to set the hook, like Susan told me. The pain, the agony, and the fear shot through my mind, and I screamed. I wanted to cut the line, but Susan said that the fish would die with all that line hanging from its mouth. I couldn't stand it. The fish was fighting and hurting itself more. I used telekinesis to pick it out of the water and hold it still. I used the same to open its mouth, and, as gently as I could, I removed the hook. Then I healed the fish and let it go. I threw the fishing pole in the pond and reeled in Susan's pole. I took off the hook and tossed in her pole also.

Julia and Aggie were shocked. Susan said, "Well, I guess we won't be doing any fishing."

Patricia floated up out of the water. "Hey, you guys drop something?" She saw the look on my face and dropped the two poles back into the water. "Never mind." She went back under the water.

I looked at Susan, "What is she doing in the pond?"

"Colleen decided that the belts and helmets should be tested in saltwater and fresh water."

"Oh. Let's go back to camp now. I think I've had enough of fishing."

Julia was continually writing. Her mother had to take her by the arm and start her going.

After a while, Julia said, "Freddy, how did you feel catching that fish? You looked like you were in pain." Julia saw that I was about to tear up, and she put a hand on my arm.

I said, "I'm sorry for the way I acted back there. To answer your question, I felt everything that fish felt, including all the pain and fear. It felt like my gut was being pulled out. I put my shields up, but it was too late. I already knew. I had to stop the agony."

Susan stopped and put a hand on my hair. "I'm sorry, sweetheart. I should have thought. You can't stand to see or even think of something or someone getting hurt. It never dawned on me that fishing would be the same or worse."

Julia pulled back a little, as if something sad just crossed her mind. "You're empathic so much that you can feel when an insect dies. That is why you kept cringing every time I smacked away an insect. I was hurting them. That must be hard on you. Very hard. That's why your mother is so insistent that we stop attracting bugs. She knows. When you saved our world from the bugs, you felt the death of every bug that you killed, didn't you?"

Looking at the ground, I sadly said, "Yes."

Julia gave me a hug and said, "I'm so sorry. I'm so very sorry." She was crying, and that started me crying, and that started Aggie crying. Susan just waited for us to stop so we could continue on, but even she hadn't realized the impact that killing the bugs meant until now. Susan kept a sympathetic hand on my shoulder until we reached camp.

It took me the rest of the day to cheer up, but I did and the remainder of the two weeks went by without a hitch. The bugs stayed off Julia and Aggie and out of my hair. No one else had problems with the equipment, and it worked well in the water. It even worked great to stop damage from a shark attack.

Some of the team members made a bet with Betsy. The bet was one hundred dollars that they could find her anywhere on the island within one hour. Susan agreed. Betsy smiled and took off the belt and helmet, saying, "Let's

see how good this equipment truly is. Find me if you can."
She took off. The team gave her a two-hour head start. It
took over six hours to find her. The sneak was in her tent,
sleeping. No one thought to check the camp. As she told me
later, "Freddy, there is no substitute for skill and brains. And
I'm not a klutz!" She thumped me on the head.

"Ouch!"

After that, we went to Mars, though not the domes. We
went to the sandy craters, and the team flew all over the
place. They used every aspect of the equipment, and it all
worked great. I had made ships that fly faster than the speed
of light; weapons that destroy fleets; robots; great computer
systems; energy sources that are cheap and renewable; and
the AutoDoc, and these girls were more impressed with
this equipment than all the rest. Go figure. We packed up
and started heading home, but something was whistling
through the air like a bomb dropping.

✦

Gray asked Red, "Can you duplicate that equipment? It
is far better than anything we have."

Red said, "Some of it. I suppose we could make it vampire
style, if you want, but his energy source eludes us. I must
say it is far superior to anything we have."

Gray said, "And you say this openly in front of him."

Little Yellows said, "Why not? They will know soon.
They downloaded all our information."

Gray said, "True. That was a disastrous tactical error
and may give a powerful species more power. They are not
fools, you know. Green, please continue. We have little time
before his reinforcements arrive."

CHAPTER 31

✦ ✦ ✦

ATTACKED

Before we could pack up everything, warnings and alarms sounded, and shields went up. I instantly searched and realized a missile was headed our way. I tried to use telekinesis, but it was shielded. I yelled, "Shields up, everyone! Put your shields on max now!" One of my destroyer escorts shot down through the atmosphere and blocked the missile. The impact, as the missile exploded against the ship, caused a devastating blast wave that flattened most of the vegetation and destroyed hundreds of thousands of creatures instantly. Luckily, everyone was wearing the belts, and all had their shields up in time, so none of us was hurt. The small landing ship and all our gear was not so lucky. I teleported everyone to the deck of the destroyer escort, and we quickly left. A full destroyer-class ship came down to clean up the site and remove all my equipment, so no one else could get their hands on it.

On the deck of the destroyer escort, called *Harm's Shield*, I called out to K1 through my helmet. She answered, and everyone else listened in.

"Hello, Freddy. How may I help?"

"I was just attacked, and I need to know where the missile came from."

"Freddy, there is a small cloaked ship following behind the *Harm's Shield*. It is powering up another missile. Do you wish me to dispatch this small ship?"

"No, can you power down the ship and missiles and send it to the base near my home?"

"In progress. May I suggest I knock out the three people aboard?"

"Please do."

"It is done, Freddy. I teleported the ship directly to the base. I have also contacted the base commander, and there are three of your ships already there, ensuring the ship does not go anywhere."

Susan put a hand on my arm, indicating she had it from that point. She said, "K1, can you look at the scanning files and determine where the ship came from?"

"Working. It was launched from an old army base in Oregon called the Umatilla Chemical Depot. The depot was shut down back in 2015. The base was bought by a private company. The company name is not on any records I have access to. I have information from the FBI files that General Johnson, the one you disgraced when building home base, was seen there on several occasions."

I turned to Susan and said, "That ship was shielded with the same technology as the kidnappers. General Johnson may be a big part of this."

Susan said, "K1, can you search the world and find General Johnson?"

"Working ... completed. General Johnson is not found. That means he is not on the planet or is shielded in some way that I cannot detect."

Susan shook her head in frustration. "I knew we should have killed that maniac."

I touched her arm in a comforting way. "You're not to blame. There is no way you could have known." Thinking out loud, I added, "So the general is a part of this kidnapping issue and probably a big part of the attacks against me. Seems I have an enemy."

Patricia added, "The general comes from old money. He is extremely well funded."

Susan looked like she just had a thought. "K1, can you determine what funding the general has and where it is being spent?"

"According to records, the general was a billionaire several times over, and all cash has been removed from banks, all holdings sold, and the assets hidden. Except for the FBI records of him being seen at several abandoned army facilities, there are no records showing anything about the general for the last three years or any of his assets. He even sold his house and yacht."

I ordered, "K1, please scan each of those army bases, and check for recent use and shielding that could block your scanners."

"Working, Freddy. There is nothing blocking my scanning. All bases show no signs of activity for years, except Umatilla Chemical Depot. There has been a lot of activity there, but there is no activity at this time. Freddy, the ship I teleported to the naval base near home base just disintegrated with all three people on board. It was some type of self-destruct. There is nothing left except green dust."

The girls were murmuring, and Susan said, "Quiet! K1, can you do a search on the cloaking device? I need to know if it is the same as Freddy's belt."

"Working ... it is the exact same."

Susan's look hardened. All expression was gone. I backed up a bit, and so did most of the girls. She ordered, "Freddy, take us home immediately."

I instantly teleported us all home.

Susan started giving out orders for doing a search to find

the breach in security, for moving to Mars, and for sending all nonessential personnel away from the base after intense screening of everyone.

✦

Red asked, "This General Johnson—what do we know about him?"

Green checked with the Body Proper. "Master, General Johnson has never been picked up. Several others humans have been captured who knew of him but none was close to him or knew anything about him."

I said, "We are still looking for him. He is out there, planning."

Black said, "A rogue intelligent general with funding and support and is highly capable. We would hunt him down and destroy him."

I said, "If you ever find him, please do not kill him. Bring him to me."

The way I said it made all of them uneasy, and even Black backed up a little before saying, "Green, please continue."

✦ ✦ ✦

UNDERSTANDING

Packing and shipping everything to Mars went well. The problem was, we were not ready for more than just the home contingent. Having nearly three hundred specials and their families became a major disaster. The new base commander arrived and took over very efficiently. Supplies were brought in, housing was developed, and new domes went up overnight. I worked on safety issues, built my new shop, and learned how to rough it.

Becky and I seldom saw each other, and each time we did, she played hard to get. She can't fool me. Silly game. All it did was make me sad and mad and make me want to forget Becky altogether—as hard as that was going to be. I had never purposefully done anything to hurt Becky, yet she was treating me this way, and it hurt. I even saw her on the arm of another boy. I was very sad after that for several months. Colleen came into my home one day to talk with me. I was in the computer room, working on a new and highly updated computer for Home.

"Freddy, can we talk?"

I peeked out from the computer room and then walked out. "Hello, Colleen. What can I do for you?"

"Let's sit in the living room." She took my arm and led me there. One look from her, and the two team members and Cooky left, making excuses of chores and plans they needed to work on. I sat down on the couch, and she sat next to me. "Freddy, you're making a big mistake with Becky."

I was a little shocked and somewhat upset that she would bring up Becky. I asked, "Colleen, exactly why are you saying this now? I am trying my best to keep her out of my mind, and this is not making things any easier."

Colleen looked at me with one of those "God give me the strength" looks of exasperation. "Why do you think Becky is doing what she is doing?"

"She is playing a game called 'hard to get.' The game is designed to cause men to go mad, I think."

"The game, Freddy, is to make you jealous and to make you fight for her."

"Fight for her! Is she in any trouble that she did not get herself into in the first place?"

"No, boy, she is not. What she is trying to do is make you want her so much that you would do anything to have her."

I looked at Colleen as if she were insane. "And waking an entire base and commandeering a destroyer, half the team, and a bunch of specials in the dead of night to save her is not proof enough?"

"Calm down, Freddy—and don't you ever yell at me again! Becky is being silly, and I don't think the two girls who are teaching her are working for her best interest. Perhaps if she were a little stronger of an empath, she could see through their manipulations."

"So what am I supposed to do? Send her flowers or candy? I did that several times. Storm out when I see her with another man? I did that also."

"I heard. That is exactly what she wants you to do, and that is exactly why you should *not* do it."

"What?"

"Freddy, I am going to tell you a secret that is best kept away from all men. Please don't tell it to anyone else, and especially don't tell anyone I told you this. All womankind would disown me."

"I won't say a word, and I can lock it behind shields so tight that no one will see."

She put her hands on my cheeks and looked me right in the eyes. "Freddy, the best way to force a woman to stop playing games is to mimic her." She noticed the blank expression on my face and gave a big show of annoyance. "Play the same game back, you fool! If she plays hard to get, you do the same. If she plays the 'I'm upset' routine, do the same to her. She will be upset at first, but she will see what is going on and realize that playing games is not a good idea."

"You're telling me that I should waste my time hurting the feelings of some girl by pretending to be in love with her, just to pay Becky back? Anything less, and she would see right through it."

"You want her to see right through it, you dumb ox. Tell the girl you choose that the only reason you want to be seen with her is to show Becky that you don't care anymore. She will love helping. Pick the right girl, and she will take every opportunity to flaunt it. You won't have to do much of anything."

"How do I pick the right girl for something like this?"

She looked kindly at me and stroked my face. "You are so naive. I would have thought that you would have had many girls by now. It's a downright shame. You work far too hard. Pick a girl that Becky doesn't like, and slowly start showing interest. It's that simple."

"It sounds simple, and that's what makes me think it is not so simple."

"Well, you will have to work at it. If she steps up the

game, you have to also. And for goodness' sake, don't ever give in. Act happy. This is an issue of willpower. You are fighting three girls, not just Becky. Show some of that super-genius. Prove your inventiveness, and stay for the long run."

"You're asking me to go to war with Becky. How will I know if I am winning?"

"You will know. Believe me. Half the specials report to Becky. You should be able to get the other half reporting to you. They would love a game, as they are getting bored. This would give them something to do besides schoolwork and farming."

"I could do that."

"Yes, you could. Don't slow down on the improvements to this base. Goodness' sake, the new captain would be mad as a stepped-on snake if he found out I set you on this course. He would be very upset that I delayed his improvements."

"I understand. Thank you. I have a lot to think about."

She stood up. "Remember. Don't tell anyone."

"I won't."

She left.

I thought, *She was telling the truth, but she had an underlying reason to do so. I wonder what her secondary agenda is. No matter. She was telling the truth, and this gives me some ideas.* I smiled. It gives me some wonderful ideas!

Two days later, Susan walked up to Colleen. "You think it worked?"

"It worked. You were right. Telling the truth was the only way to keep his mind off leaving. He'll be so busy trying to play games with Becky, and with working on the improvements, at the same time that it will be another year before we need to worry about this again."

"Thanks."

But before Colleen could say "you're welcome," Susan was gone.

✦

Big Yellows said, "Admiral, you are needed on the bridge. We just were told by the Body Proper that a much larger fleet, with ships ten times the size of the largest one we have ever encountered, just magically appeared in our way. An entire fleet just teleported into out path. We are slowing down."

Little Yellows said, "This one just sent a message to the new ships."

Surprised, Red yelled, "Through the helmet!"

Gray asked, "What did he say?"

Little Yellows said, "He said to hold off until the actual fighting ships arrive. Apparently, all we've fought so far are old-style ships with little to no real ability. Ships that he created years ago. The real warships are on the way, and there are thousands of them."

Gray turned white. Blue nearly fainted. Black entered the room and looked at me with a need I could not identify.

Clear entered, and I watched him travel across the room as he thought about killing me. His career was ruined, and his pen was in shame due to his actions—and he was going to kill me for revenge.

As I watched, the Black followed my lead and struck with a force I had not witnessed before. He slammed the Clear, grappled it, and then broke it in two. Then he turned to me. "That coward is dead." He turned to Gray. "Admiral, as per standard orders, your color is in charge. The Body Proper is telling your leader."

Gray looked at the tank and then looked around in a panic. "Where is the prisoner? Where is Freddy?"

To be continued ...